Toe Tagz 3

Ah'Million

Lock Down Publications and Ca$h Presents

Toe Tagz 3

A Novel by *Ah'Million*

Ah'Million

Lock Down Publications
P.O. Box 944
Stockbridge, Ga 30281

Visit our website @
www.lockdownpublications.com

Copyright 2020 by Ah'Million
Toe Tagz 3

First Edition March 2020
Printed in the United States of America

Lock Down Publications
Like our page on Facebook: Lock Down Publications @
www.facebook.com/lockdownpublications.ldp
Cover design and layout by: **Dynasty Cover Me**
Book interior design by: **Shawn Walker**
Edited by: **Lashonda Johnson**

Stay Connected with Us!

Text **LOCKDOWN** to 22828 to stay up-to-date with new releases, sneak peaks, contests and more…
Thank you.

Submission Guideline.

Submit the first three chapters of your completed manuscript to ldpsubmissions@gmail.com, subject line: Your book's title. The manuscript must be in a .doc file and sent as an attachment. Document should be in Times New Roman, double spaced and in size 12 font. Also, provide your synopsis and full contact information. If sending multiple submissions, they must each be in a separate email.

Have a story but no way to send it electronically? You can still submit to LDP/Ca$h Presents. Send in the first three chapters, written or typed, of your completed manuscript to:

LDP: Submissions Dept
P.O. Box 944
Stockbridge, Ga 30281

DO NOT send original manuscript. Must be a duplicate.

Provide your synopsis and a cover letter containing your full contact information.

Thanks for considering LDP and Ca$h Presents.

Acknowledgments

I would like to thank all my fans for all the support. Much love to my people behind the wall. Most importantly, God for blessing me with such talent. My besties Vicki and Bryeshia I love y'all. Pretty P, I'm waiting on ya'. Free my brothers I love y'all. It'll get greater later. Thank you to the ones that showed me love on Amazon. I hope you all continue to ride out with me. Cash, thanks again it's a movement, let's go.

To my loyal fans, I know you've been looking for me on social media to see the face of the artist who's penning all of this heat. Unfortunately, you'll have to wait until I'm finished serving this bid. Until then, you can reach me at:

S.Hawkins #1999583
742 FM 712
Marlin, TX 76661

Ah' Million

Ah'Million

Prologue

Skkrr! I couldn't move quick enough as I pulled up and hopped out in front of the low-class hospital.

"Hey! Hey! Please, somebody help, my brother got shot! I yelled to no one in particular, at the few stragglers splattered around the parking lot, but it was as if no one heard me. A few slowed their stride and a couple gawked in my direction, but no one rendered aid.

I rushed to the rear of the car while Bando rushed to my side as we struggled to pull Mun out of the backseat, a terrified Kadejah darted past us and into the hospital to find help.

Bando and I struggled to place Mun's limp arms over our shoulders in an attempt to guide him inside the hospital. His body felt like a trash bag full of soaking wet laundry.

"Aarrggghhh, I can't—fuck!" Mun yelped out.

Bando and I quickly removed his arms and laid him on top of the pavement.

"I'll be back!" Bando hollered jogging into the hospital.

Mun peered up at me and smiled through blood-stained teeth.

"I missed you, man," he whispered in between coughs. His eyes fluttered as he struggled to keep them open.

Bando came rushing back out of the hospital with several medical staff members on his heels. "Come on let's get him on the stretcher!" one of them yelled.

"We have to put you up here, bruh," I said tugging at his shirt, Mun didn't respond. "Mun! Mun!"

"Come on we have to get him inside now," The doctor demanded as him and the rest of his team circled Mun's body.

"one, two, three," they counted in unison lifting his body from the compound.

"Mun," I whispered as the tears welled up in my eyes.

I couldn't lose my brother again. I followed the team of doctors inside while constantly yelling Mun's name. The doors to the emergency entrance flew open and we headed straight to the trauma room.

"We have a male, several bullet wounds to the chest, abdominal, and shoulder." I stared down at all the blood that covered Mun's clothes.

"He's not responsive! Wait, he has a faint pulse!" The doctor yelled. "Sir we're going to have to ask you to leave," he continued.

I stood there in shock, not knowing if I should leave or stay. I didn't want to go, leaving Mun alone to fight for his life.

"Sir," the doctor repeated calmly.

I continued to look past him, watching the other doctors attempt to resuscitate Mun. I slowly turned around and headed for the door. I couldn't see no more I begin to recap my mother's last days.

"I love you, Mun" I mumbled as I made my exit.

Chapter 1

Arianna

Don't trust anyone -- not your best friend or even your wife!
Micah 7:5

"Yes. Can I have a medium iced coffee, Hazelnut creamer, and Cappuccino with one slice of pound cake and a blueberry muffin please?"

"That will be three dollars and eighty-five cents. I'll bring it to you shortly," I stated.

"I need a medium iced coffee with Hazelnut creamer and Cappuccino, Amy!" I yelled while removing the fresh pastries off the tray.

"Coming right up!" Uncle Pank decided to get a coffee shop instead, he figured me and Kadejah needed more of a homely environment. Having the two of us employed meant we'd stay out of his pockets and off the streets. We practically ran the place, it was just four of us, Amy, Dan, me, and Kadejah. PJ helped if someone took time off, but usually, between the four of us, we would cover for one another. The store opened at 5 a.m. and closed at 5 p.m. Once the school year starts back Uncle Donk agreed to hire one more employee.

My life had changed drastically since moving in with Donk. I couldn't ask for anything better. Not only did he support me financially, but he was like the father I always wanted. So attentive and caring I made sure to express my gratefulness, whenever I was given the opportunity.

"Have a blessed day," I said sitting the pastries and coffee in front of her. I didn't know who the lady was, but I did know that she came quite often, but with a different order.

"Arianna!" I jumped in terror at the sound of my name.

I relaxed seeing that it was just PJ since everything I'd been through these last few months it was as if I was waiting for trouble to come knocking on my door.

"What?" I asked rushing towards PJ and Kadejah who were standing at the door.

"Karisha having a pool party tomorrow."

"Boy, I thought something was wrong. So, is that why y'all have shopping bags?" I asked eyeing him and Kadejah's bags.

"Yeah, we picked up a little something. I got you a bathing suit," Kadejah said heading towards the back.

There were two separate rooms in the back. One was Uncle Donk's office, the other one belonged to me, PJ and Kadejah.

"Amy, cover for me please?" I asked making my way to the back.

Amy was a white chick. She was older than us but younger than Dan. She acts like the promiscuous woman God warns us about in the Bible. However, she worked hard, just green as hell. She was pretty stacked to be a white girl. I think she got that mommy make-over surgery. She didn't get those D-cup breasts and fat ass from her mother. She loved Uncle Donk but he paid her no mind.

Dan, on the other hand, was an older guy who loved to bake. He once owned his own bakery, but one of his employees accidentally started a fire and burnt the entire establishment down. Uncle Donk used to always buy pastries from his bakery so when he found out what transpired he found Dan. Dan was a man of God he hummed and sang gospel songs all shift. He never griped or seldomly asked questions. He just did his own thing. Other than his glass eye, due to a terrible car accident. He was peculiarly handsome. Although his colorless iris was a bit scary.

"Close the door," Kadejah snapped.

Tru had really been stressing her out lately, I wish she was released already. One minute, Kadejah was joking and laughing the next minute she was going off and throwing things.

"I'm telling you it's something up with that lady out there. I can feel it. I don't trust her," Kadejah spoke while I locked the door to the office.

The office was quite spacious. Kadejah and I wanted to paint it pink and decorate it with Cardi B posters, but PJ objected. Since we were all fans of Lebron James we decided to do a Lakers theme.

Toe Tagz 3

Kadejah's desk was a tad bit bigger than me and PJ's. Uncle
Donk did his best to treat us equally, but we all knew Kadejah was
the pick and she always got more. Honestly, I didn't have a problem
with it, I mean she is an actual relative.

"Why you say that?" PJ asked kicking his feet up.

"She always here and it's this look she gives me. It's not a,
"Well, I'm just enjoying coffee and soaking up the A/C" her eyes
are always roaming, swiftly and her ears are always perked."

"Perked?" I cut in.

"Yes, perked. Ever paid attention to dog ears when they think
they've heard something?"

I burst out laughing at Kadejah's insinuation. She was always
very attentive, she rarely missed anything, but this time I thought
she was mistaken.

"Man, you buggin," PJ stated removing the shoebox from the
Gucci bag.

"Alright don't sleep on her. I'm going to leave it alone, but I'm
going to tell Dan and Amy to keep a close eye on her once the school
year starts back."

"Alright, whatever. Check these out, Ari," PJ said removing the
lid on the shoe box.

"Ooohhh, those are nice PJ," I praised eyeing the new cream-
colored Gucci low tops.

"So, how you cop those and that fit? Uncle Donk gave you extra
money?" Kadejah nosily interceded snatching the Versace frames
off her face.

"Don't worry about me. Y'all depend solely on Donk. I got my
own shit going on."

"Yeah, the last time you did your own thing we all almost ended
up dead, nigga," Kadejah shot back rolling her eyes.

A few months ago, PJ supposedly tried selling dope, but it back-
fired. He was robbed and owed the plug a tremendous amount of
money not being able to pay it back, he turned to Uncle Donk for
help, but it was too late. The plug and his hittas came looking for
blood but ended up covered in blood.

One of the hittas turned out to be Uncle Mun, who was the last man standing. That is Donk's first brother who went missing for a while and everyone assumed he was dead. Kadejah, who decided to take matters into her own hands snuck through the back, spotted Mun, and shot him several times assuming he was the enemy. That night Mun flatlined but came back and today he's fine, and I mean fine.

Uncle Mun and Donk were alike in many ways only at times uncle Mun was oddly quiet. Anytime we were all out in public he constantly looked over his shoulders.

"See?" Kadejah asked holding up the hot pink cheetah print one-piece bathing suit.

"Yes, I like it—but maybe it's just a bit too revealing. Don't you think?" I hesitated before placing the polyester material up against my skin.

"There you go with that bullshit. That's why I didn't get you one like this," Kadejah teased pulling the ocean blue, gold, and black two-piece cheetah print bathing suit from the shopping bag. "Ooohhh, Kadejah it's beautiful, but Uncle Donk not going to let you wear that."

"He's not going to know I'm wearing it." She smiled at me devilishly.

"He'll be mad if you go behind his back, Dejah," Arianna added.

"You not prancing around in that thotty shit in front of all them niggas!" PJ protested.

"What you going to do, tell? If you do, I'm going to tell exactly how you got that extra money," Kadejah threatened with a smirk.

"Hold on, what's that? Do y'all hear that?" I asked looking around the office.

"What is that?" Kadejah joined in.

Knock! Knock! Knock!

"Don't just stand there looking crazy open the door," PJ demanded I quickly unlocked the door while rolling my eyes. PJ's arrogant ass always had something to say, I was so over him.

"I don't mean to interrupt, but that girl is here again," Amy said barging in and shutting the door behind her.

"Okay! Why your scary ass running in here and shutting the door? Watch out!" Kadejah fussed bypassing Amy and out the door.

PJ, Amy, and I followed suit. As soon as the door to the office opened, I could hear the extremely loud ranting in broken English.

"Say—say," Kadejah spoke softly

"Uh-uh, where is Bando's ass? My friend Keesha's baby sister Ri-Ri says she saw his car up here ten minutes ago!" Liz yelled Liz was Bando's issue, supposedly his baby mama.

He hooked up with her at a party one night and claim to have gotten pregnant. She's been a pain in his and everyone else's ass since finding out she was with child. I've never met a ghetto and ratchet Hispanic girl in my life until I met Liz. She even wore box braids with weave. Surprisingly this was her first pregnancy, so hopefully, she'd just be very cautious.

"Look I been letting you come down here with all that bullshit and I been keeping quiet because you're pregnant, but bitch you got one more time to raise your voice in my place of employment and I'm going to demolish your wack ass," Kadejah spoke firmly and calmly.

"*Wack!* Who you?" Liz yelled.

Her eyes bucked in fear and she abruptly got quiet, once Kadejah charged her, thank God PJ grabbed her in enough time. I quickly stood in between both ladies while PJ tried calming an angry Kadejah.

"She's pregnant, Dejah. Chill, you just got out,' PJ said

"Liz just leave and if I see Bando, I promise to tell him you stopped by and to give you a call.

"And his ass better call!" she yelled from the foyer quickly backpedaling and nearly tripping over her feet.

"That bitch don't want no smoke. You saw how she got quiet when I walked up on her. Ol' scary-ass!" Kadejah cursed.

I stood by the door and watched Liz swerve off the lot making unintentional eye contact with the lady who ordered the blueberry muffin. She smiled and I smiled back, yet I saw the look Kadejah had just warned us about.

How long had she been gone? How much did she see? Why was she just parked out front? I thought.

Chapter 2

Persuasia

"Which cuh-lar you like"? The Chinese lady asked peering up at me.

Esha and I sat beside each other in the nail shop, reclined in the leather chairs while receiving pedicures. Lately, we hadn't been able to relax because things had been so hectic.

Ring! Ring! Ring!

Esha quickly answered her phone using her palms to balance it against her ear. She mumbled into the phone, I slowly looked out the window at the activity outside the shop.

"I want the same metallic gold you used on my nails," I responded. The petite nail tech walked off to retrieve the color. I couldn't help but notice her bite-size ass. "Who was that?" I pried as soon as Esha moved the phone away from her ear.

"Oh, it was um—one of my regulars," she hesitated.

"Bitch quit lying" I knew when Esha was lying because her left eye twitched.

"What I have got to lie for? Come on, P, you're the slick one. When are you going to tell me where you were last night?"

"I was with a bandit." I giggled.

"*A bandit*? What did he steal?"

"My soul, bitch"

"Damn, it was that good?"

"Yes, Lawwdd!" I felt crappy for sleeping with the enemy, but then again, he left me and there are no limits when it comes to a hurt bitch.

"You always holding out. I don't do you like that, Persuasia."

"You always whining, hush!"

"So, then tell me, you already gave me a hint." I deeply exhaled while staring directly into her eyes.

"Nobody," I mumbled. I couldn't form the words. I didn't trust Esha, so I continued to lie.

"Come on, please," Esha begged.

"Drop it, bitch."

"That's some hoe shit, P", Esha spoke with venom.

"I'm aware of that, but whose side are you on?" I asked.

"Definitely not Donks," she quickly shot back. "Get the getting, while the getting is good. I ain't mad at you.

Can I have Mun?" She inquired cheerfully before tossing her hair over her shoulders.

"Hell, nah! I fucks with my brother in law and I'm not about to be in the middle of that."

"Whatever, so are y'all progressing? How long y'all been sex-ing?"

"What do you mean progressing?"

"Are you considering anything more than sex?"

"Slut, hell no! Donk not going to kill me!"

"I know that's right." The Chinese lady lifted my foot from un-derneath the water, examining it while speaking loudly in Vietnam-ese.

"Uh-Uh, don't talk shit in your language. Talk that shit in Eng-lish," I voice loudly. She peered up at me dumbfounded and I met her gaze.

"You have anything lined up?" Esha asked while looking down at her phone. She was trying to hide her smile, but she was doing a poor job.

"No, I was actually going to ask you the same thing."

"Nope, but I'm working on something, something worth the wait."

Chapter 3

Donk

"What's up?" I greeted Bruce as he climbed into my black G-Wagon.

"Hey, man, I have good news and bad news," Bruce mentioned.

"Run it," I shot back peeping the scenery outside my window.

"I found out who the chick is, but it's not sufficient enough to figure out Tim's location being that she or her grandmother no longer stay there. The girl's name is Mariyah Washington, she used to reside at twenty-one, sixty-six Checota Drive with a severely ill grandmother."

"Okay, that's it?" I asked evidently disappointed in the useless information.

"Pretty much she had an older brother that resided there as well, but he's deceased. Supposedly he was murdered many months ago."

"Hold on. Where did you say she stay?"

"Twenty-one, sixty-six Checota Drive," he repeated.

The shit hit me like a ton of bricks. "Meech's little sister?" I thought aloud, but how did she get into the club unnoticed. Tim couldn't tell this bitch was sixteen?

Full of disbelief, I couldn't deny the state of shock, I was in. It was evident, I didn't believe in leaving witnesses behind, but I knew the grandmother wouldn't be an issue.

Who would've thought a fifteen-year-old girl who wasn't even home would come back and bite us all in the ass? I thought. "Fuck!" I yelled hitting the steering wheel.

"Wait, you know this girl?" Bruce inquired peering at me.

"Yeah, but that's not important, I need to find Tim."

"I'm trying Donk," Bruce retorted rubbing his head in frustration.

It looked like Bruce hadn't slept in days. The large bags under his eyes sagged like an elderly woman's breasts.

"Look, man, this is what I pay you to do. You got two more weeks and that's it." Times like this made me miss my longtime friend and private investigator Jeff.

Hopefully, he made it to the Heavens. Obviously, someone had been playing Jeff at his own game. Surprisingly, they won. He was poisoned on a cruise ship. All I know is he was found in his room seated at the table face down in a bowl of spaghetti. Police don't know if it was an employee or a tourist.

"You betcha two weeks is all I need," Bruce responded quickly lifting his head up in hope while sticking his hand out. I balled my fist and we bumped fists instead.

"Alright, I'll see you soon," he stated while climbing out of the truck.

I logged onto my Instagram and scrolled to Tim's page so I could watch the video again. It was the last thing he posted on his page. Tim had been missing since the night he was released. I assumed the Mariyah chick was the one glued to his side all night. I peered closely at the chick who was in and out of the video as I studied the young girl intensely. I concluded why Tim fell for the okey-doke.

Her makeup was flawless, the bright eye shadow and heavy foundation added years to her baby face. Her body was fully developed. The only thing that probably would've exposed her young age, was perhaps her conversation which I'm sure was minimal seeing that Tim was pissy drunk. Bando and Chris were in and out of the video a lot as well. I paused the video getting a closer look. Her grey eyes were phlegmatic and held no emotion. If only someone had been paying attention, shorty looked out of place. Times like this made me miss Quaylo. Apart of me believed Tim's dead, but I'll be damned if I give up like I did with Mun, until I see him with my own eyes. I'm going to be looking high and low for him, dead or alive.

Beep! Beep!

"Donk! Donk!" The kids called out.

"Can we have a dollar for the ice cream truck?" They yelled while running up to the driver's side of my whip. The rugged-looking and nappy head kids took turns begging as I parked in front of Esha's crib.

One night me and Quan went to the club and it just so happens that Esha was one of the dancers who came running to the V.I.P section once the DJ announced our arrival. I was already a bit tipsy, but after the four shots of Henny, I was seeing double everything. Esha took charge dragging me away from the women that crowded around me and led me to the Men's bathroom. She wasted no time unzipping my Prada jeans and pulling them down along with my briefs. She admired my mans and planted kisses all over it.

I banged and beat up her tonsils until I came, releasing semen on her bold eyeshadow and mink lashes. I guess that's why I'm at her place, right now for the third time this week, cause her lip service was just that superb. No lie after the run-in me and Esha had at the club that night. The next morning once I sobered up, I felt a twinge of guilt knowing the bond between Esha and Persuasia, but that lasted no more than 5 minutes. As good as I had been to Persuasia that bitch should have been extra careful with me. I knew I loved her cause I had yet to broadcast or bluntly put the shit in her face. Eventually what's done in the dark comes to the light, it's just a matter of time.

I hopped out of my G-wagon and hit the alarm. One thing I loved more than anything was kids, it's a shame I don't have any of my own. It was at least six to eight of them huddled up with their hands out. I gracefully handed each one of them a five-dollar bill not just making them smile, but me smile as well.

Quickly saying, "Thank you." They all took off toward the ice cream truck.

I noticed one of the kids who goes by, Lil' Rob wasn't so quick to move. "Thanks again, Donk," he stated before heading into the opposite direction.

"Hey, you good lil' man?" I called out before he was out of reach.

"Yeah," he quickly shot back

"Come here." He slowly turned around and walked toward me with his hands shoved inside the dingy basketball shorts.

"Huh?"

I bent down until we were face-top-face. "Man, tell me what's up. I know there's something on your mind. You're usually the first one to take off."

He kicked at the dirt a few seconds before responding. "I'm saving up every dollar I get to get a haircut and buy me some new kicks. Every day the kids at my school tease me from the time I get in, to the time I leave out," he explained.

I looked at his clothes and the worn-out sneakers and instantly felt sorrowful at the boy's misfortune. I felt his pain, I knew his struggle. I always stressed to Kadejah on the importance of counting her blessings and to appreciate even the little things, cause it's someone who's always in a harsher predicament. I peeled two hundred dollar bills off the top and sent Lil' Rob on his way.

A few seconds after he walked off, he stopped and spun around. The corners of his mouth were turned down and tears welled in his eyes. He ran toward me full speed and wrapped his arms tightly around my waist. "Thanks, Donk, for always caring about me," he said with strong sincerity.

Before I could respond he released his grip and headed back down the street in the opposite direction. Moved by his sudden show of affection, I watched Lil' Rob until he was out of sight.

"What's up?" I asked making my way inside Esha's crib.

It wasn't anything close to lavish, but it was very neat and clean with a flower-like scent.

"Heyyy, Boo!" she responded enthused. "I fried fish and shrimp with coleslaw, along with macaroni and cheese on the side. You hungry?"

"Hell yeah, but I don't want too much of that coleslaw." I frowned.

"Boy, I can cook but fuck you. You don't have to eat my shit," she voiced playfully walking into the kitchen.

Suddenly, the song *Hot Girl Summer* by *Megan Thee Stallion and Nicki Minaj* played loudly from Esha's iPhone, which so happened to be lying beside me. I peered over at the screen which read, *P. my B.*

"*P. my B?*" I thought as Esha came running around the corner wearing a distraught expression.

"What's up, bitch?" she coolly answered. I couldn't hear what the person on the other end was saying so I just continued to watch Esha closely.

"Uh-uh, bitch, I'm not at home right now!" she lied.

Whatever the person on the other end of the phone said, seemed to put Esha at ease. Her contorted face was now relaxed. I didn't have time for all the extra weird shit she had going on, I just wanted my tool sucked. I agreed to link up with Mun in a few.

"That was close," Esha voiced sitting the phone on the table.

"What you mean close? Who was that?" I inquired.

"That was, Persuasia. She just got done at the beauty shop and wanted to swing by."

"Oh, that's P. my B?" I repeated aloud.

"Yeah, Persuasia, my bitch."

I moved my eyebrows up and tightened my lips. The nerve of these chick's man. When it comes to good dick or long money, loyalty goes out the window. God forbid if it's good dick and long money, they'll be ready to kill.

"Alright finish making my plate I have somewhere to be in thirty minutes."

She smacked her lips before returning to the kitchen. Not even five minutes later she was standing beside me with a plate of food and glass of Kool-Aid. I took a sip of Kool-Aid before diving in.

"Damn, girl this shit's sweet as hell. Can you add a little water to this shit?" I ordered looking ugly as hell with the sour expression on my face while I held the glass up.

Without a response, Esha grabbed the glass and did what I told her to do. I was looking for a hint of anger but found nothing. I swallowed the catfish nuggets whole. It's been a minute since I fried fish and that shit was good than a motherfucker. I was licking the ketchup from my thumb when Esha unzipped my jeans. I slightly lifted my ass cheeks off the sofa allowing her to easily pull down my jeans and briefs. She sniffed around my shit then begin to do it discreetly, while holding it with one hand.

"Why you always do that?" I asked curiously.

"Duck butter."

"Duck butter? You got me fucked up, ain't nothing nasty 'bout me or my dick—wrong nigga," I shot back

"Nah, I'm just checking for me it's a habit. I just end up getting lost cause you smell so good I like to savor the moment."

"Whatever come on with it," I demanded reclining against the massive pillow that decorated the sofa.

Esha gently grabbed my mans with both hands gawking at it admirably as if it was a piece of gold while gently massaging it. She rubbed her soft massive lips along the tip and the edges before placing it into her warm mouth. My body stiffened as I prepared for what was yet to come. Immediately after she started, I relaxed and enjoyed every second of her performance. I looked into Esha's eyes through grunts while controlling her head with my left hand.

My head fell back in complete bliss while I let Esha do her thing. Two nuts later I was standing inside Esha's restroom using one of the clean washcloths to clean my dick. I tossed it in the dirty laundry basket before exiting.

"You gone?" She called out as I bypassed her.

"Yeah," I replied while fishing around in my pocket.

I quickly peeled off six-hundred-dollar bills and tossed it on the table.

"When am I going to see you again?" She asked following behind me.

"I'll hit you up, Esha," I replied a bit annoyed.

"Cool."

I opened the door to her crib and hopped in my whip.

Chapter 4

Persuasia

Esha had been acting real weird, but I'm trying to give the bitch the benefit of the doubt. She's up to something, if I find out she's chasing that sack without me I'm cutting her ass off. One thing about my cut off game—it's strong and she knows it. Yeah, she was quick on her toes with her response, but I picked up on the hesitation. Me and Esha were the best of friends, but even the closest have issues.

Years ago, back when I was in high school. My high school sweetheart Jamal's birthday was approaching so I wanted to go all out.

One day after school I sat on the passenger side of his Impala and I asked, "Bae what do you want for your birthday?" He looked at me while slowly approaching the red light. "You not going to get in your feelings?" I scowled curiously.

"I want a threesome." He continued staring into my direction as if he was awaiting a response. "Why would I be in my feelings?" He zoomed through the green light.

"Hellooo, Jamal?"

"Cause, I want a threesome with Esha." I was completely stunned, and left aghast by his comment I remained silent while I battled with my inner thoughts.

"My best friend? How long has he been lusting after her? What's the need for two? Am I not good enough?" I thought.

"Persuasia!" He voiced loudly.

"Huh?" I asked gazing straight ahead as if I was in some sort of trance.

"You asked me, and I told you. Is it a problem?" he asked.

"No, I'll make arrangements." In spite of being disgusted, I didn't want to tell Jamal no.

Jamal was three years older than me and his money was as long as a retired businessman. He took care of me and my mother and he was all mine, so I thought. Once Jamal dropped me off that night, I called Esha and asked her if she'd be down.

"Hell nah, that's your dude and you're like my sister," she retorted.

"Please, Esha," I pretended to beg.

"Bitch no!" she repeated.

Well, that bitch no! Turned into loud moans that Saturday night at the Omni hotel. I'd never been so uncomfortable in my life. I stood off to the side while I witnessed in pure disdain my dude of two years fucking my best friend's brains out. At first, he positioned me in different positions to keep me involved, but after he tried forcing me to eat Esha while she sucked him I nearly gagged. As soon as I rolled out of the way, the two got busy excluding me as if I didn't exist. My blood boiled as I watched them attack each other nonstop. He fucked her like he fucked me, and she fucked him back. I sipped on the Ace of spades until I passed out. None of us ever mentioned the threesome again, not to each other anyways.

Almost six months later, my Samsung was pressed against my ear as I tried calling Esha, but she wasn't answering. Esha stayed about five minutes away, my mother let me use her car that night and since the night ended early, I decided to stop by Esha's, who was on punishment and couldn't hang out.

I bypassed Esha's and noticed her bedroom light off, so I kept going until I spotted Jamal's starter Jacket hanging from the tree outside of her window.

"What the fuck?" I mouthed astonished.

My heart pounded while malicious thoughts invaded my mind. Nearly hitting a parked car, I realized there was nowhere for my mother's Chevy Malibu to fit so I parked dead slap in the middle of the street and hopped out. Walking as swiftly as I could, I slowly lifted the window high enough so that my head could fit through. I lifted one of the blinds and peeked in.

It was as if I was having Deja Vu and we were in the hotel all over again. Only this time I was standing outside a window watching the two people I loved the most go at it like newlyweds on their

26

honeymoon. Silent tears cascaded down my face, as my blood pressure begin to rise. I wanted to cry, I wanted to hop inside the window and kick both of their asses, I wanted to ring the doorbell and alert Esha's mother, so she'd find Jamal and beat Esha's ass.

However, I did nothing. I was so dispirited, I couldn't even cry. I backed away from the window and hopped inside my mother's car. After that night I never spoke to neither Esha nor Jamal again. The death of her mother seven months later reunited us. She made a vow to never betray me in that way again, and I made a vow to myself to never choose someone I know to have a threesome with me and my man.

I believe Esha will betray me again, that's just the way it is. I just don't believe she'll betray me the same way twice.

"Bry, I'm outside. Come on," I spoke into the phone.

Me and Bry were good friends. I met her taking PJ to daycare one morning. She griped and whined to me about her deadbeat baby daddy. He was just like the majority of these men, who sell drugs for a living with no goals, plans, retirement or legal help lined up. Soon life takes a toll and you find yourself broke, extinct, or locked up.

His mother wasn't any better she hit the club more than the both of them. She was a fifty-one-year-old grandmother with a pill and gambling addiction. She cursed like a sailor, engaged social media beef and pull-ups. No lie her pull up game was strong until one day she pulled up to fight the wife of the married guy she had been having an affair with and she unloaded the clip on her ass. Luckily, the lady was blind in one eye. She hasn't pulled up on no one since then, because of all that Bry was left to pay the sitter fees on her own.

Eventually, it became overwhelming and she was in dire need of some bread. I invited her to one of my private parties. I host at this small building that I rent for parties and certain occasions. Bry was a natural, she was a bit green to the pole work, but she didn't miss a beat twerking that ass. Recently, she quit and found a job at the hospital in the respiratory field which she had been attending school for while dancing. Esha and Bry got along on the strength of me, but they really disliked each other. Esha felt as if Bry was lame, and Bry felt as if Esha was trashy, but they kept things cordial around me so I never commented on anything.

"Hey, boo, you remember Shaniece, my little cousin?"

"Hey, girl!" Shaniece waved. Shaniece was a bit on the chubby side but her face was gorgeous. I hadn't seen her in a minute, yet she still looked the same.

"What's up chick y'all ready?" I asked from the driver's seat of my car.

"Yeah!" They shouted in unison.

I couldn't help but notice Shaniece's ass. I know it had been a year or two since I'd seen her, but I don't remember that booty. Last time I saw her, that ass resembled two flour tortillas, now it was poking out like elbows. I silently nodded my head discreetly admiring Shaniece's new look.

"This ho better be lit!" Shaniece shouted

"Hell yeah, 'cause I would've preferred to Netflix and chill anyways," Bry chimed in.

Bry was a bit conservative compared to the rest of us. I'm surprised she agreed to come out tonight.

Ring! Ring! Ring!

"Turn that down real quick, P," Bry requested as she answered her phone.

"Hello?"

"Hell, No! I'm on my way to the club Tonya. I don't care, I'm not even in my car! No, Tonya, sit your old ass down somewhere." *Click!*

I peered over at Bry she was definitely irritated.

"Who was that?" I snooped

"Girl, my child's grandmother."

"Ms. Joyce?"

"Hell no, my mother is a lady. That's Tonya's ratchet ass!"

"What's her issue?"

"Same ol' shit, the new guy she been hanging with is married. Well, he been hiding for a few days and now she's ready to go fight the wife because she feels played. Supposedly he's been telling her that they were about to divorce."

"Fight the wife?" Shaniece and I asked in unison.

"Yes."

"That's that woman husband!" Shaniece chimed in.

"She's looney," I said.

"Baby lets go turn up I'm not worried about her," Bry said placing her phone inside the cupholder.

The nerve of these women. I thought as I pulled up to Park Avenue.

The line was longer than loop 12 and there was no way in hell me and my bitches were going to stand in it.

"Hold on, hol—" The bouncer said placing his arm out in front of us.

"Got damn, y'all looking good as fuck," he continued, licking his lips.

"How much for skip line?" I smirked.

"Y'all just go right in." He stood to the side and me any crew mobbed inside.

"For real? We been standing out here for hours!" The chicks in line called out.

"And you gon' keep standing!" I yelled before walking in.

"Okay, keep that same energy. Talk that shit once I get in!" she hollered.

I kept it moving, bitches always underestimated me because of how I looked. I wanted her to come in here with that bullshit.

DaBaby's *Bop* played inside the spacious yet packed club. Niggas was everywhere. Bum dudes, Ballas, stunnas, and niggas that danced harder than females. The club wasn't as elegant as I thought it would be, but it was far from a hole in the wall.

"Excuse me." The slight brush against my ass compelled me to look back.

"Twan? Damn, baby what's up?" I greeted.

Twan looked enticing, he was drippin' no doubt and he wore a black and white Givenchy fit with a pair of lime green and black Balenciaga's.

"Damn, Persuasia, that is you. You still looking good. You at DG's?"

"Nah, K. O. D." I eyed Twan lustfully

The last time I'd seen him he was chubby as fuck trying to hustle and go to school. He really wasn't a street nigga, so no one treated him as such. He was more like a flunky. Twan had been sniffing behind me like a lost pup for years, but I just never gave him the time of day.

"Oh, okay, P. I'll see you around," he stated walking off.

I was taken aback by his sudden reaction. I wanted him to stick around so I could know more about this, *new* Twan that stood before me, but he wasn't even sweatin' a bitch. I grabbed him by his arm ceasing his movement.

"Who you here with?" I asked

"A couple of my niggas"

"Can we catch up?"

"Maybe later, put your number in here," he said handing me his iPhone II.

Damn this the one with the three-camera lens in the back. I don't even have this one yet. I thought.

Da Baby and Lil' Baby - Baby came on, and Bry and Shaniece ran to the dance floor. I wasn't here to shake ass. I was trying to scope. Me and Esha was doing a little more than dancing nowadays, the club just wasn't enough money for us, besides I wanted to show Donk's ass I was just fine without him. Trying to out-do Donk, support my habit, keep up with the latest fashion, and support my son. I needed to keep the cash pouring in.

I hated to admit it but luckily P.J. had his own shit going on. I was still trying to figure it out, but I wasn't going to drive myself crazy trying to do so. I was sitting at the bar nursing a drink. To anyone else you probably would assume it's a glass of Patron, or maybe just something clear and fruity. It was just water. If I wanted to land something, I was going to have to be quick on my toes. Out of my peripheral, I saw Shaniece approaching. She flopped down on the empty stool next to me.

"What's wrong, bitch, you don't like this song?" I asked

"Yeah, this my shit," she replied dryly using her pinky to move the side bang out of her face.

"Then what's the problem? You over here looking all sad and shit," I said.

Shaniece just kept shaking her head as if nothing was bothering her.

"Shaniece," I called out.

"What, Persuasia?" You want to know my problem? This is my motherfuckin' problem!" She yelled smashing the cushioned but shaped pad onto the table.

"Bitch, you had on a booty pad?" I chuckled nearly spitting the water out of my mouth.

"Yeah, girl, I was over there twerking on this dude. I had him pinned on the wall throwing this ass when he tapped me on my shoulder and pointed at my back. The damn pad had moved from my ass all the way to the center of my back. I ran to the lady's room embarrassed and snatched the motherfucker off," she stated seriously.

I was laughing so hard I had tears in my eyes. My stomach ached like I had did 1,000 sit-ups the shit was so funny. I was still laughing.

Shaniece peered at me and said, "Oh, that's funny bitch?"

"I mean, Shaniece, why would you wear that to a club? You should've never got on the dance floor if that's the case. "You know a nigga going to get behind that or grab that."

"You right."

"You never thought about surgery?"

"Hell yeah, I just don't have the money."

I glanced in Twan's direction. "Maybe I got a job for you."

Ah'Million

Chapter 5

Lil' Tim

The stale stench of musk and mildew was making my stomach queasy. I couldn't believe I'd *got caught slippin'* and by a young bitch at that. I knew Mariyah as a beautiful and innocent adolescent, but that part of her had vanished and birthed a demon. Months ago, Donk, Bando, and me ran up in her grandmother's house and killed her brother Meech for fucking with Kadejah. Mariyah which is Meech younger sister was at school at the time. So, we thought.

Months after his death I found myself at Big Chris's spot with a gun pressed against my skull. Initially, I assumed it was Chris's fat ass. Seconds before I felt the steel, I noticed a picture of him and Dino on his shelf. Dino was the op, Chris tricked me into believing he was against Dino, but that was all a lie. At the time I really didn't understand, but now it all made sense. Reggie tried to warn me, but I didn't take heed.

I couldn't tell the time, but I could somewhat count the days. I could tell by looking through the small 5x8 window when it was morning or night. When the sun would rise again, I counted it as one day. It took me quite some time to realize it, but since I've been keeping track, I know for sure it's been more than fifty days. Believe it or not, I have not seen one person up close since then. Sometimes, I can see people walking past the small window from a distance. I've tried banging, yelling but nothing works.

I washed my ass, dick, and armpits a few times, but I have yet to take a real shower. Hours after being down here I awoke to two massive bags of dog food and three normal size buckets of water. One of the buckets is what I used to wash my hot spots the other two I just been slowly sipping on. I also been nibbling on the extremely hard dog food trying to be conservative as possible, now I'm down to just a corner of the bag. Yes, I've been eating this shit.

It's actually not that bad. I can't tell you what it tastes like, I hold my breath while imaging I'm eating a box of Cap 'N Crunch or Sugar Smacks. I drank the last of the water yesterday. I began to lick around the rim of the bucket as well. I searched every corner of this room, but there is no way out. The concrete floor tells me it's a garage, but with merely a glimpse of light, it's difficult to pinpoint anything.

Is that rain? I thought as I quickly stood to my feet to look out the small window. Rain my ass. "Get away from here with that!" I yelled banging on the window at the stray dog.

His leg was cocked as he was pissing on the ground directly under the window, a few drops landed on the window. He jumped slightly when he saw my fists, then quickly dropped his leg and sniffed around and up and down the window. He even licked it, dogs were fucking gross. He began to dig up dirt underneath the window and it finally clicked, that this dog could possibly be my way out.

I pressed my face against the window hoping he'd just go harder. I remembered the little dog food I had left I ran and dug my hand deep down into the bag and grabbed a handful before retreating to the window. I pressed my hand against the window exposing the dog food. The dog sniffed the window as if he could actually smell the dog treats. He began digging again, I could hear his whimpers but the sound was faint. I was starting to get dizzy and discouraged so I leaned against the wall for support.

"Hey! Hey! Get away from there!" I heard a guy call out.

I couldn't see the man because the dog was blocking my view. The dog didn't move. I could hear footsteps approaching, and I became jittery. I pressed my face against the glass ignoring the physical state I was in. I swallowed continuously trying to gather spit to soothe my dry throat, but it wasn't working.

"Get away from here you mut!" he hollered kicking the dog in the side.

The dog howled and scurried away, then with all the strength I had left, I yelled at the top of my lungs while banging on the thick glass. I could see the guy peering around through squinted eyes while he strained to hear what direction the noise was coming from. I continued to bang, but it was useless. The guy turned to walk away. I quickly scanned the ground. I instantly spotted a rusty pipe and raced to retrieve it. It was heavier than it looked, yet I gave the pipe one hard thrust against the window. The second time made him stop dead in his tracks looking me directly in my eyes.

I dropped the pipe and pressed my face against the glass as I mouthed the word, "Help."

He quickly removed his phone from his pocket. As he placed the receiver to his ear, his mouth moved swiftly but I couldn't make out anything he was saying. The comfort of knowing I had finally been discovered put me in a state of shock. I thought I had stopped breathing for a moment.

I awoke in a hospital bed and scanned the room swiftly. My throat was dry and itchy, and my eyelids felt like quarters were sitting on top of them.

Is that Kadejah? I thought.

"Kadejah?" I strained in an attempt to yell but it came out merely above a whisper.

She jumped tossing the jacket that covered her face to the side. Although her face was covered, I could spot Kadejah from anywhere.

"Heeyyy, Tim! I missed you sooo much!" She yelped cheerfully wrapping her arms around my neck.

The smell of tangerines and Peaches caught my attention and instantly I wrapped my arms around her waist. I rested my nose in the crane of her neck and remained still for a moment as I enjoyed her scent and presence. I pulled away in an attempt to let go, but Kadejah swiftly pulled me back in tighter.

"I love you, Lil' Tim," she spoke softly in between sobs.

"Kadejah, you crying?" I asked forcing myself out of her embrace.

Tears poured down her innocent face and it only gave me more of an urge to pull her in closer. I repeatedly kissed her forehead until I heard laughter escape her lips.

"You slobbing, move!" She escaped, only to see tears falling from my eyes as well.

"Aww, you crying?" She smiled inching closer.

"Move girl, I really missed you. I thought I'd never see y'all again."

Donk walked in with snacks in his hand, his eyes grew twice their size seeing his face lit up my insides.

"What up, baby!" he yelled overly enthused.

"My nigga! I was just telling Kadejah how much I missed you."

"How long you been awake?

"Not that long. I spotted Kadejah's little ass sitting over there." I cut my eyes at her discreetly catching her roll her eyes, she hated when I called her *little*.

"All bullshit aside, who's first on the list to go? I want to know all the details," Donk requested taking a seat.

"Well, first of all, Chris wasn't who I thought he was. He was in cahoots with Dino the whole time. I don't know his motive or plan for sticking around, but the night I was released I left the club with him and a bitch. When we get there Chris was directly to the back, he claimed he was just gathering a few things to leave. The chick told me she was going to freshen up.

"I was feeling good admiring Chris's bachelor pad when I noticed the club picture on his shelf. It's a group of dudes, including Chris and Dino who were standing beside each other. So, I peered a little higher and saw more pictures of them as well as a copy of Dino's obituary. I was so awe-struck by the betrayal and disbelief, that I didn't hear anyone creep up behind me until I felt the steel at the back of my head. I'm not going to lie, I did beg Chris for my life until the chick spoke, and I realized it wasn't Chris. It was Meech's fifteen-year-old sister.

"Don't actually remember what happened next, I just remember waking up on a cemented floor eating hard ass dog food and drinking water out of a bucket. A dog happened to be playing in the yard by this small window I could see out of when a guy made him move. The guy noticed me and immediately got on his phone."

"Damn, you been through it. I spoke with this P.I. a few days ago and he informed me about the girl, surprised the fuck out of me. I got him working on her whereabouts."

"Bet, cause her ass gots to go."

"No doubt."

"Hey, who knew you and Reggie were going to Tyler?" Donk asked.

"Me, you and Bando. Why?"

"Well, I spoke with a friend who was coping from Reggie that night, and the brief description he gave me sort of matched ol' boy Chris who was on the video you posted on your page," Donk revealed.

I peered straight ahead trying to remember and suddenly it hit me.

"I did tell Chris, uh, as a matter-of-fact, I spoke to him on my way to Tyler," I admitted, shaking my head.

"That nigga killed Reggie, fam."

"You're right. I was careless and Reggie warned me, man."

"It's all good, they're gone now," he said.

Ah'Million

Chapter 6

P.J.

Bubba sat behind me in the backseat bobbing his head while mumbling lyrics under his breath.

"Boy, get your biscuit head ass on!" I roasted Bubba.

Bubba was one of the three members of my squad. Bubba and I were the same age, but he chased the bag like he was an older cat. Bubba was a bit hotheaded, he felt like he had something to prove due to his size. He stood 4'10, 120lbs. Although he was short, he fought hard and he was quick as lightning. He had a red complexion and sandy red hair that he kept edged up with the name *Lil' Phat* cut into one side, in memory of the murdered rap artist. A few freckles were here and there on his perfectly round face. His chipped front tooth didn't stop him from pulling hoes. His crooked smile was the perfect fit for his rough personality.

"Boy, you ugly then a ho' get yo—" Bubba started.

"Aye man y'all niggas play too much. We sitting outside this spot getting ready to pop out at any minute and y'all playing. One day that playing gon' have you somewhere you don't want to be," Trigga chimed in.

Trigga was the oldest out of the bunch, four years older to be exact and he pretty much kept shit organized. He sort of resembled the rapper Wiz Khalifa minus the dreads. He rocked big plaits like O Dawg from Menace To Society. Trigga didn't take advantage of the fact we were younger and green to certain things. He gave us the game along the way and made sure we didn't get lost in the hype. Days I would say fuck school or days me and Bubba would be lit and doing stupid things for money, Trigga would tell us the real. So, real I'd feel lame for not taking heed. I never tripped cause I knew it was all out of love.

"Fuck it let's just go in already. We seen the bitch leave an hour ago. She maybe on her way back now," Bubba chimed in.

"I just got a feeling someone else's in that bitch, but fuck it come on," Trigga said grabbing the duffel bag under his seat.

"Hold up, like I always say—we all come together and we're leaving together or die trying. We not going to be in here no longer than ten minutes. Empty-handed and all that's cool, we'll live to shake something else rather than take our chances standing in one spot and end up jammed up or dead. Til the tagz."

"Til the tagz," we spoke in unison dapping each other up.

We all hopped out of the black Ford Escape at the same time shutting the doors. It was a few minutes after eight and the sun still hadn't risen. Today Bubba and I supposed to be at school but we'd been peeping this lick for weeks now and today was perfect. I figured I'd miss the first class, but I'd make the next one. I still hadn't thought of a lie for Donk, before I even make it home the automated system is going to notify him of my absence today. The neighborhood was quiet and empty. A car or two bypassed but paid us no mind.

Knock! Knock! Knock!

The Duffel was by our feet as we waited anxiously to see if someone would answer.

"Y'all stand right here, since no one's answering, I'm going to look for a way inside to avoid kicking the door in and awakening the neighbors," Trigga insisted.

"Bet." Bubba pulled the Newport from behind his ear and lit fire to it.

"Nigga, you look like a box of Newports, with yo' water jug head ass. Put that shit out," I voiced. *Whack!* I slapped Bubba at the back of his neck.

"Why yo—what's up. I'm bout' to kill yo' shit, with the square in my mouth," Bubba stated posting up.

I followed suit and before I knew it we were slap boxing right outside the front door.

"Bro, what the fuck?" Trigga whispered loudly with his hands on top of his head certainly irritated.

"Y'all lil' niggas not coming with me no more fo' real, fo' real," he continued.

"Man come on Trigga," Bubba plead breathing hard.

"Just come on, I found a window."

40

We walked around the side of the house as Trigga lifted the already ajar window. Trigga eased in first, Bubba was next, then me. I could hear music blaring throughout the house and I peered over at Trigga and Bubba confused. It was clearly someone home.

Why did we come inside? I thought.

"What's the plan?" I whisper.

"We gon' all stick together, bust if need be. We gon' try to go unseen. It's a safe, or stash spot with at least fifteen to twenty grand. We need to find it, let's go," Trigga stated leading the way.

We begin to search the room we climbed into. It was usually where you least expected it. I was so nervous I couldn't even stay focused, knowing someone could walk in at any second made my nerves bad. I barely opened the door and poked my head out sitting on the couch in the living room was a heavyset, dark-skinned dude playing a video game. He was reclined back on the sofa looking like he didn't have a care in the world.

"Aye nothing's here let's move," Trigga said, my eyes grew wide hearing his request.

I slowly opened the door to the room and we quietly but swiftly filed out one at a time. I was scared as hell, all dude had to do was turn his head. It wasn't like we were behind him we were merely down the hall. Another door rested down the long corridor and we quickly darted down the hall and inside before being spotted. This room looked more like the master's bedroom. A huge portrait of the female that left earlier and the guy in the living room covered nearly the back of the entire wall. Luckily, this room was neat making our jobs easier.

"Okay! So, you gon' creep up on me like that?" I jumped at the sound of his voice.

My heart was beating out of my chest as I began to think of the possible consequences that were subject to come, only to turn around and see dude in the same spot peering at the TV screen. A sigh of relief escaped my lips. The adrenaline rush had me moving swiftly. Drake blared so loud throughout the house I wasn't worried about him hearing us whatsoever. I flipped over the mattress and looked under the bed while Trigga removed every painting and portrait from the wall. Bubba searched the restroom that was connected to the bedroom, but neither of us had found anything yet.

"Man, we have to go to the next room," Trigga announced looking defeated.

"Let's look around a little longer then we'll move. We have to search everything thoroughly cause it's no redo. Fuck 'round and this nigga catch us," I said while looking in the dresser.

"You right."

I was passing gas left and right I was so nervous. Lowkey, I wanted to check my briefs.

"Aye family I found it," Bubba said carrying the Fila shoebox.

"Damn, she had that shit in a shoebox?" Trigga asked whipping out his pocketknife and removing the duct tape.

"I was expecting to find a safe or something," I said

Trigga lifted the lid revealing the small pistol and several rolls of money.

"Bingo. We'll count this shit in the car."

"Bet," Bubba and I agreed.

Trigga eased the door open and we slid our way out. I nearly bumped into Trigga trying to locate the dude, but he wasn't in his original spot. Trigga stopped moving altogether, he was so shocked. Although he was nowhere in sight the music continuously blasted at an extremely high volume.

"Come on!" I yelled as I quickened my pace towards the room we initially started in.

What if this nigga knows we're here and he's somewhere waiting on us with his pistol? I thought, sweating profusely.

I could see a light illuminating from underneath and in between the cracks in the door to the left when I heard a toilet flush. We all rushed inside merely a second before I heard the bathroom door open.

Without exchanging words, we quickly hopped out the window one at a time. I was a bit afraid to go last, hoping I wouldn't be the one he walked in on. Once my feet hit the pavement, I was still a nervous wreck as I jogged to the truck, looking back while doing so.

"Five racks a piece? I'm cool with that. One of y'all can have this little ass deuce-deuce," Trigga capped.

"Get that ho' P.J. you the only one who don't got a burner," Bubba suggested.

"Shit, I'm not trippin' cause it's pink. I like it," I said holding the .22 in my hand.

"So, what's the plan? What y'all' trying to get into tonight? Trigga asked.

"I want to turn up, let's go to the strip club," I replied

"Fuck it lets mask up and get some more cash," Bubba suggested. Good just wasn't good enough for Bubba.

"I know five gees isn't enough when you have an impeccable swag, but we gon' chill man," I said.

"Alright bet." Bubba smiled.

Ring! Ring! Ring!

It was Arianna.

"What's up?"

"Where you at?" she inquired.

"Why, Ari?"

"Quit being mean and just answer me."

"I'm handlin' business why?"

"You want to go to studio movie and restaurant?"

"Nah, I'm going to the club with my niggas.

"The second I stop sweating you, you're going to miss me."

"Bye, Arianna. I love you!"

Click!

Arianna is a trip, but I knew how she felt about me. I respected her if nothing else. She had become fam. Since I'd been chasing the bag her level of importance has dwindled. I'm really doing her a favor. I know I can make her mines and creep around with these hoes too, but I love her too much to give her anything less of her worth. I decided to leave her alone until I'm ready, she'll be there.

"Hold on before we head out let me call my momma to make sure she's not working at all tonight. It was pointless to ask her which club she'd be at being that she bounce from club to club.

"Hey, ma?"

"Yeah, baby"

"You working tonight?

"No, I might go to bed early."

"Okay, just checking, I love you.

"Why?"

"I love you, ma!"

Click!

I was lit, and I'd be damn if I let her blow my high with 21 questions.

Kevin Gates - Hard For was playing as we bopped through the door. The cabaret was live and I was ready to see something. Bubba wanted to go to this other strip joint in South Dallas. It was something like a hole in the wall. The hoes had fucked off ass shots, war wounds, bad weave, missing teeth, and one was pregnant. Yeah, the dice game was live, Kush had it so foggy you could barely see but I was feeling a different atmosphere tonight.

Since Bando and I had been hanging I start clubbing. The first time he took me to a strip club I was hooked. Donk and Persuasia didn't seem to have a problem with it, so I was determined to show my face every chance I got. The knots in my pants had them fitting a bit too snug. Wasn't any pressure with wearing tight pants everybody shit was tight nowadays.

Money green and peanut butter Yeezy boots matched my stone island coat. The black Fendi Momento watch decorated my wrist, but I wasn't using it to tell time. Sloop foot I swaggered slowly through the club. Trigga and Bubba were on the side of me. Bubba dressed lowkey, burgundy Polo sweatsuit with a pair of black foam posites. Trigga wore a supreme hoodie, light denim Guess jeans, a few diamond chains, and a pair of black Timberland boots. His hair looked a few days past due, but his edge up was on fleek. I moved through the crowded club smoothly winking and licking my lips at all the chicks that looked like something.

To my surprise, it was a lot of those. I got mad respect cause everyone knew I was kin to Donk, Persuasia's name held weight in the clubs as well. The club setting was lit, and I was ready to get in the mix. Bubba wasn't quite aroused by the club scene, he'd rather be out on the lurk, right now. I'm surprised he didn't stay in the car.

"Hey, Fam, give me the keys. I'll be out in the car!" Bubba screamed over the music. I had spoken a bit too soon.

Trigga gave him a smirk before tossing him the keys to his Yukon. I always told Bubba that spirit of greed would have him in the system or a body bag. He would always say, *"Til' either happens, I'm gon' chase that sack."* I don't even bother preaching anymore. The only other thing Bubba loved more than money was music. He promised that if he gets enough money, he can pay for a beat from someone known. He was interested in *Mike Will Made It* and *Zaytoven*. Maybe pay a hot artist to feature on one of his songs to get his name and music out there. Trigga's goal was to own his own club/tattoo parlor. I hadn't made up my mind yet.

I was also the only one who really didn't have to be in the streets. Donk took good care of me and if I needed something, I could ask him for it. Now that Mun was back, he showed mad love, too.

The yella bella on stage dancing to Megan Thee Stallion Big Ol' Freak had me mesmerized. I was entranced by her measured movements to the beat. I reached into my pocket, removed the knot, and threw half of it on the stage. Five hundred ones rested in each pocket. I would've thrown all my money if it was on me, that's why I made sure to bring only what I wanted to throw.

If I leave with my pockets flat as pancakes it wouldn't matter. The song came to an end, shorty snatched her money up from the floor, and left the stage. I started after her to ask for a lap dance but the chocolate drop coming on the stage made me change my mind. That bitch came from behind the curtain looking like a Hershey's kiss, I could've just walked up and taken a bite out of her sexy ass.

"Hey, y'all tonight's her first night. Show some love to Chyna Black. Y'all know this girl black and sexy! Shawty looks good enough to eat, huh?" The DJ joked.

He started laughing, but if he felt anything like I felt then I knew he was serious.

"Look like you going to need some more ones," the light-skinned cute chick said after I tossed the other half of one's onstage.

"Nah, it's more where that ca—" My words were caught in my throat when I saw Persuasia storm right past me.

I slowly walked behind her, while following her with my eyes. She headed to the V.I.P. section and I was right on her heels. I could tell in her stride and disposition she was livid, but I had to see what the fuss was about. My eyes grew twice their normal size once I spotted Esha on her knees with her lips wrapped around Donk's man. He was reclined back in his seat listening to my mother rant and rave.

"Oh, yeah, Esha! Bitch, you supposed to be my best friend. This why you been acting funny, hoe?" Persuasia hollered lunging at Esha.

I quickly stepped in between them before she connected with Esha's face.

"Esha, dang you know you dead wrong," I commented holding my mother back. It wasn't as easy as I thought it would be, she was stronger than I thought.

"Fo' real Donk, to this extent?" Persuasia asked with tear-stained cheeks.

"Excuse me, P.J. Persuasia, when you did what you did all loyalty and respect, I had for you left, too. I told you a long time ago you didn't have no fucking friends. Matter of fact, since y'all so cool get down here with yo' friend and feast on this beast together. Table for two!" Donk shouted.

My nostrils flared and my palms begin to sweat. I really wanted to get at Donk's bitch ass, but I learned a long time ago to choose my battles wisely.

"Come on, Ma," I spoke pulling her shirt, but she wasn't moving. I couldn't stand there a minute longer and watch her hurt. Tears continued to pour and her bottom lip trembled.

"Nigga, I'll kill you," I threatened clutching the .22.

Donk reclined back and laughed. "The only reason you still standing is cause I know you not gon' pop shit. Security, show these two the way out!" Donk ordered.

I was furious as I stood there motionless mugging Donk. I wanted so badly to seek revenge for my mom, but I couldn't bring myself to kill a man that I loved like my own father. The team of security swiftly dragged us out. Donk and I locked eyes until we were no longer in each other's view. After today I knew the family would never be the same.

Ah'Million

Chapter 7

Mun

Kneeling beside my mother and sister's tombstone saddened my spirit as I sat the bouquet of roses down. Since being released from the hospital I'd made it my business to visit the cemetery once a week. I felt a lot more connected this way. Life's good, but it can also be a bitch. On several occasions, I'm being followed but no one has made a move. I know it's Juanito, I was one of his bodyguards in Juarez, Mexico.

Recently he decided to visit the states on a business trip. The initial reason for the trip was to clean up some dirty money with a few legal investments, but once we made it here his son informed him about a drug exchange gone wrong, petty war if you ask me. Something Nesto could've handled on his own, but me and my crew volunteered our services because we had nothing better to do.

Thinking the shit was going to be simple as talking a hoe out her panties, it was the total opposite. Everyone on my team died but me, only to later find out I was at war with my own people. My motherfucking brother. I had been forced to stay away from, and out of contact with. I had been kidnapped by my old plug Donatello who wanted to avenge his niece Danielle's death. Donk killed Danielle because she put CPS in my life and we almost lost Kadejah for good.

While I was out in Jamaica with my main bitch, who I dated for 2 years named Bre. Come to find out she was crazier than the chick from the movie *A Thin Line Between Love And Hate*. She wanted all my attention, time, and love. Her sole plan was to kill me, but she ended up getting killed by the hands of Donatello. Having his own intentions to torture and kill me slowly, he decided to sell me to a kingpin he was close friends within the drug business who resided in Juarez, Mexico to be exact. Supposedly Juanito needed a cold, bloody killer. He sold me for double the price he was initially offering being that I was a fool with the tool and could sell water to a fish.

The only promise to seal the deal was for me to remain in Mexico with no contact with anyone from the states, and for Juanito to keep me as one of his until he was put in the grave. For the longest, I tried poisoning Juanito cause I knew that was the only way I'd be free indeed, but it never worked. Usually, I wasn't allowed to travel to the states when Juanito would go, but after seven years, I had finally won his trust. I had no plans of contacting Donk who was all the Fam I had left. Me and Lil' Tim wasn't related by blood but we were so close we should've been.

The day me and the other two guys went on the mission with Nesto, I didn't think I would end up in a battle for my life, but I did. My sharp thinking is what kept me alive. Instead of me looking into the barrel of a pistol. It was the opposite, but once I realized the op was my flesh and blood, we been thugging since Kadejah almost took me out thinking I was the enemy, by the grace of God I made it through. I have yet to see or be contacted by Juanito, but I know he's the one who's been watching me. Little did he know I was ready.

"I love you, Quaylo. I love you, Rochelle. I'll be back next week if it's in *God's plan*," I quoted standing to my feet.

The wind ruffled the Louis Vuitton Hawaii style shirt. The cool breeze hardened my nipples, but I didn't bother to button up my shirt. I carelessly flaunted the expensive artwork that covered my body. I remained motionless, slowly peering around the empty cemetery. Usually, Donk would be here with me. He had business to tend to and agreed to meet me here. Thirty minutes had passed and still no sign of Donk, it was time to peel out. Through narrow suits, I could see Donk's truck from a distance, so I slowed my stride. As the truck neared, I noticed the plates that suddenly threw me for a loop.

Donk plates are custom, I thought.

I removed the Dolce and Gabbana Square sunglasses to get a better look at the black G wagon. The truck sped up a little and the windows on the driver side begin to descend. Like a two-time loser running from the laws, I took off in the opposite direction. The bullets rang out and I quickly belly-flopped onto the soft, moist dirt.

Bullets whizzed past my head lifting dirt, I was a sitting duck. Although I had my burner in the pocket of my cargo shorts, I was no match for the truck full of goons.

Sskkrr!

The sound of screeching tires instantly caught my attention. Pistol hanging out his truck Donk immediately let his ratchet spit. The men in the truck returned fire. I scurried to my feet, hid behind a massive tree, and fired rapidly at the gunmen. Like a cat with nine lives Donk hopped out the whip, twin tech's in each hand letting them rip. The piercing screams told me more than one had been hit. I jogged towards Donk still bussin' my Glock. I assumed the driver was hit when the truck recklessly crashed into a metal pole.

"Let's see who sent this nigga!" I yelled jogging towards the smoking truck.

I opened the door to the driver's side and the gunmen were slumped over with his head resting on top of the steering wheel. I removed the black ski mask and grabbed the guy by his stringy hair to get a good look at his face, but his lifeless eyes told me he wouldn't be giving up the man who called the hit. Donk was rummaging through the back as I leaned over to check the dude on the passenger side, no pulse.

"They both dead, bruh," he confirmed.

"Yeah, these two are too. That faggot Juanito is behind this shit"

"Maybe, maybe not. Juanito's the truth and these was some amateur ass niggas. You supposed to be dead. Shit the way I hopped out like Queen Latifah on *Set It Off* I'm supposed to be dead, too."

Donk was right, with the money and power Juanito had I supposed to have been dead. But if it wasn't Juanito who else would want my head?

Ah'Million

Chapter 8

Kadejah

I got wind of what transpired between Persuasia and uncle Donk. The past two days were a bit odd without P.J. He was acting like he wasn't bothered by the sudden change, but I knew he was lying. I tried talking to Uncle Donk on P.J.'s behalf but he wasn't trying to hear anything I was saying. The look he gave me actually scared me, so I dropped the topic.

PJ and Persuasia were upset with how things went down but I didn't understand the big deal. I was always told to act accordingly to the way you'd like to be treated. Persuasia did some hoe shit with that stunt she pulled. You're tied to a boss, but you're steady shakin' ass in the club as if you need it. I'm glad he cut her off, but today she came in good use.

Tru and I had been making plans for me to visit her, but since I didn't want an adult to accompany me, I needed a fake I.D. that's where Persuasia came into play. It only took an hour but the whole ride there was quiet. Now we were sitting in front of the detention center.

"You need me to wait so I could take you home?" Persuasia asked looking in my direction.

"Nah, I'll catch the bus. Ain't no telling how long the wait is, thanks for asking."

"You good, look despite what's going on with me and your uncle. I grew to love you, Kadejah. I still and will always love you and whenever you need me, I'm coming."

Persuasia words really touched me, and at that moment all the hate I had for her vanished.

"That means a lot to me, P. Thank you I'll call you later to let you know how it went," I assured hopping out of her smoke grey Buick Lacrosse.

I zipped up my Nike hoodie and headed towards the building. The lot was full, and a few people lingered throughout it. As I entered the facility, I was nervous as hell seeing the variety of authority. Some were dressed in street clothes and a few were uniformed. I walked towards the sign that read *Visitor's Section* and took a seat in the lobby. There were males and females of all sizes. I sat around awaiting any familiar faces from when I was locked up, but I didn't see anyone, which was a good thing.

"If you're here for a visit come forward," the lady inside the picket announced. I walked up to the window with a few others on my heels. "I.D., please. Who are you here to see?" she asked.

I could feel the sweat beads form across my forehead as I handed her the fake I.D. "Lytrice Oshae."

"What is your relation?"

"She's my cousin," I replied. The more I lied, the more I began to sweat, now I could feel it in between my ass cheeks.

"Okay, Ms. Richards, she'll be out in a few have a seat in the lobby."

I stood there motionless in disbelief. *Is this it?* I thought.

"Next!"

"I guess so," I mumbled taking my seat.

It felt good to be on this side of the detention center. I walked over to the vending machine, I wasn't hungry just nervous as hell.

Shit! Is that Woods? I quickly hid on the side of the vending machine letting him bypass.

I was sure he saw me but the freshly manicured nails, natural face beat, and twenty-six-inch bundles were far from the kinky ponytail and jail scrubs.

Nah, he would have certainly said something if he saw me. I thought.

I bought a bag of jalapeno Cheetos and took my seat. I was a nervous wreck as I waited to see Tru, after a few minutes the lady inside the picket slid up the window.

"Ladies and gentlemen in an orderly fashion walk into the visiting area and go to the empty room you see your visitor standing in front of. You have thirty minutes."

I quickly walked through the door and swiftly scanned the crowd. As soon as I laid eyes on those hazel green irises the pace of my heartbeat quickened. She looked like she'd lost ten pounds since the last time I saw her, but other than that she looked the same. She flashed the biggest grin I'd ever seen, and I quickly made my way to the door. The officer closing the door to our room looked unfamiliar, I'm just glad it wasn't Mr. Woods.

Once the door was closed Tru grabbed me by the waist as I wrapped my arms around her neck. She grabbed my round face giving me the sweetest, softest, most passionate kiss I ever witnessed. Her tongue tasted sweet like candy as grunts escaped her mouth.

I let her take control, I softly sucked on her bottom lip before pulling away.

"Bae, chill and let's chop it up. They think I'm ya cousin," I said.

"Okay, I'm sorry I just miss you so much, mama"

"I know, I miss you, too."

"So, what they saying? Why haven't you been released, Tru?" I asked curious. I just couldn't understand for the life of me why she was still here.

"Supposedly I have to do a little more time because I wasn't granted all my back time."

"Exactly how much time, Tru?" I asked raising my neatly arched brow.

"Just five to six months."

"*Five to six months*, Tru, really? You said that like it's five or six days. I need you out here with me!" I whined. I was beyond pissed this was the last thing I wanted to hear, but as she peered at me with those beautiful hazel eyes. I quickly softened. "I'm not tripping those few months are going to fly by. I'm gon' hold you down even if it was five or six years," I assured.

The grin on her face told me she was ecstatic and in disbelief all in one. It had been merely weeks and I was losing my mind without Tru. The thought of five or six more months irritated me. I thought by now we'd be riding off into the sunset, living happily ever after. A wrench had been thrown in those plans. Tru loved me for me and those days we spent in Juvie were sweet as a getaway vacation in Cancun. We laughed and reminisced for the remainder of the time. A tear escaped Tru's eye when the officer announced the five-minute warning.

My heart saddened and I realized how hard it was going to be to walk in a separate direction once this visit is over.

"You know I love you, right?" Tru asked gazing into my eyes.

My bottom lip trembled. "Yes, yes, Tru."

"No matter what these people decide to do with me or if you decide to ride or not. Kadejah you was the best thing that ever happened to me and it was an honor to meet you. When you left, I beat myself up for being incarcerated when I could've used this time I spent locked up, looking for you."

"Tru, why you talking like I'm not going to see you again?"

"I don't mean to come off like that. I'm just telling you what's real and on my heart while I have the opportunity."

"Time's up!" The C.O. yelled on cue.

Tru and I leaned over the small round table and held each other hands for dear life. The doors begin to slam one at a time as the officer made his way down the line. Once the sudden realization hit, we leaned in for a peck of intimacy, affection, anything to express the love that lived within us.

A simple, *"I'll be missing you."* But in all actuality, there was no simplicity in the quick gesture. Once my lips found Tru's it was as if an electrifying shock shot through my body and I didn't want to move. I quickly jumped back when I heard the door next to us slam. The last thing I wanted was to get caught kissing and be restricted from seeing her again.

"I love you cousin!" I shouted once the door to the visiting room opened, but anyone with eyes could see this was no ordinary love.

"Come on, Oshae!" The guy yelled at a motionless Tru.

I stepped out into the hallway waiting for Tru to step out as well when I spotted Mr. Woods coming through the door.

What the fuck is he doing here? I thought

I swiftly looked around the room, but there was clearly nowhere to hide. Tru looked my way, noticed my uneasiness, and peered at me through curious eyes.

"I love you, I have to go," I whispered taking off in the opposite direction I had to move quickly before I was spotted.

Damn! I caught Woods glancing at me through narrow slits and I knew I was busted.

"All visitors give one last wave to your family and walk out the door up ahead to your left," he announced.

The other guy escorted the Juvies in a separate direction while they formed hearts with their hands and blew kisses on their way out. Tru and I locked eyes and exchanged sweet nothings until we were out of each other's sight. The line for the outside visitors finally began to move and I tried to slide out, knowing Woods had been staring a hole in my head for the past few minutes.

"Ma'am can I speak with you for a minute?" he asked sarcastically.

"May I help you?" I asked dumbfounded.

Mr. Woods surveyed the area before speaking. "So, how were you able to get a visit, Richards? You're not seventeen," He pried with his hands on his hips.

"Can I answer this some other time? I have to get going, sir."

He inched closer hovering over me. "Oh, so you want to play? It's only one way you could've got in here."

"Mr. Woods, okay, you know. So, what you asking me for? Is there anything else you want from me?" I asked with attitude, Mr. Woods was handsome but annoying as hell. He took his simple position too far.

"I'm gon' run your ass in if you keep bumping like you running shit."

I rolled my eyes and looked around the empty visitation area carelessly.

"So, you're really serious about Oshae?" He inquired with a look of disbelief on his face.

"Yes, sir I am. That's my friend and I told her I was going to hold it down real bitches do real shit."

"Girl, what yo' young ass know about being real?" He asked with a boyish grin.

"I know a lot, cause I've been through a lot. You always bringing up my age, so I take it that it's a problem? Since it is why you still sweatin' me?"

"Oh, I'm sweatin' you?" he mocked licking his juicy lips.

"Oh, you not? Well, I'm out," I said before turning to walk away.

"Aye take this and hit me up. Hit me up asap. By the way, I don't want to see you up here again. Next time I won't be so nice." He winked handing me a card with his name and number on it.

What he didn't know was once I put his number to use, he wouldn't have to worry about *catching* me up here, cause he'd be willingly bringing me.

I'm not leaving my bitch for nobody, I thought.

I looked down at the card before tucking it inside my bra. *I'll shoot him a text once I get inside.* I made a quick exit before running into anyone else who might notice me. The cool breeze slapped me in my face as soon as I stepped out. I quickly zipped up the thin jacket and headed towards the bus stop.

"Fuck!" I yelled peering ahead at the city bus that had just zoomed past me. I looked around while crossing the street trying to quickly get to the stop to see how long I would have to wait on the next bus. "Thirty-six minutes?"

It was freezing and the last thing I wanted to do was wait, but I didn't want to bother Persuasia, nor did I feel like explaining to Uncle Donk. Uncle Mun might be too 'noid to come anywhere where police are gathered. I sat down on the bench pulling my knees into my chest, while I watched the cars pass. I could hear my phone ringing in my pocket, but I was too cold to answer.

A green Yukon blasting loud rap music passed and the guy in the passenger seat looked directly into my eyes, but I paid him no mind. I became alert when I noticed them making a U-turn.

"Ma, you need a ride?"

"Nah, I'm good," I quickly shot back.

"Man, don't be scared it's just me and my little bro," he said letting down the back window to prove his statement.

"I want to get to know you. I'm not going to bite," he continued.

"I feel you but I'm okay fo' real, fo' real."

The two guys were Latino and the driver looked appeasing.

"Man, you want a nigga to beg, huh? It's too cold to be beggin'."

"Actually, I don't want a nigga to beg. I'm just waiting for this one-sixty-five to come so I can get home."

"*One-sixty-five*, you stay in the Grove?"

"Yeah."

"Me too, come on boo hop in. I got you," he said.

I looked around, pushed back the sleeves on my jacket, and looked at the time on my MK watch. I still had twenty-two minutes to wait.

Fuck it. Without responding I peered around cautiously then climbed into the truck. The inside of the truck was dark and smelled like grade A weed. It was so dark inside I couldn't tell what either of them was wearing. *Gunna - Drip Season 2* mixtape blared through the speakers.

I looked down at my phone that was dying by the second, with only 12% left. I shot a message to PJ with a description of the truck, the guys inside, and the license plate number that I memorized when they made the U-turn.

"So, ma what part of the Grove do you stay in?"

"Lake June and Elam, like you're on your way to Balch Springs."

"Oh okay, cool. What's your name?"

"Dejah. Yours?"

"Nando."

Ah'Million

Chapter 9

Persuasia

"Give me about ten minutes to freshen up and I'll be ready to break you off white boy," I teased closing the door to the small restroom.

Since the little run-in with Donk and Esha I been on a spree. If I wasn't dancing, I was boosting, robbing, and whatever else to get a check and stay busy. Through it all, I was lit. Pills and powder had become my addiction and I loved it. I teased the tight curls that hung freely down my back while stalling for time. The middle-aged firm owner was in position but Shaniece wasn't responding to my calls. Since finding out about Esha's disloyalty I replaced her with Shaniece, being that Shaniece was broke she had more hustle and ambition.

"Come on, Shaniece," I whispered while pacing the floor in the restroom. I stood still to cease the sound of my Christian Louboutin heels clicking against the floor.

"You have reached the v—" I was so tired of hearing this white lady when I was trying to contact Shaniece.

"Are you okay, honey?" My client asked from the other side of the door.

"Yes, here I come," I responded. *Guess I'm on my own*, I thought.

"You look amazing," he slurred once I stepped out of the restroom.

"I see you've had one too many drinks. Care for another one?"

"Yes, but after you give me a sample, baby," he said handing me the anal beads.

I looked on in disgust. Men were worse than women when it came to that gay ass shit. "Oh, you a freak-freak?" I slowly and seductively walked towards the bed.

The black bodysuit I wore hugged my body like a latex glove, and I battled with the idea of leaving it on or removing it. He lay sprawled out on top of the queen size bed grinning like a Cheshire cat.

"Get on all fours and scoot to the edge of the bed," I demanded calmly as I picked up the lube from the table of goodies. In one swift motion, he climbed to his knees. "Arch ya' back." I spread the lube on my index and middle finger and slowly glided my fingers up and down the crack of his flat ass. A few pimples decorated his butt cheeks almost making me throw up.

"Please satisfy me and quit teasing me," he begged.

Shoving the beads in an inch at a time, I watched him squirm while the annoying grunts escaped his mouth. My phone was tucked away inside my bra on vibrate. I was hoping like hell, Shaniece would call at any second and tell me she was outside the room, so this madness would end. I filled him up with deep, long strokes while I plotted on ways to break his pockets and break out all in one.

It was starting to smell a little, but I kept doing my thing.

"Yes! Don't stop, Thick Stallion!" he hollered.

Thick Stallion is my business name. The small container of Visine caught my attention, so I sped up the pace to finish him off.

"Ooohhh, yeessss—please give it to me, don't stop."

I ignored his cries and within seconds cum shot out of his small, pink penis which was pointed directly at the bed. Breathing heavily, he fell back onto the plush pillows that were scattered on the bed.

"Can we have that drink you promised?"

"Yes, ma'am."

I walked over to the table where the Visine sat and quickly poured the drinks. Continuously rambling to keep him from watching me. After pouring the brown liquor into the glass in one swift motion I dropped two drops of the liquid inside his drink.

"Come here," he ordered.

I walked to the side of the bed where he was laying when he began to stroke his penis and sip his drink.

"Here," he said pointing at his limp penis. The color resembled a pack of drumsticks in the frozen section.

"What you want me to do?" I asked playing dumb.

"Suck me, bitch!" he yelled.

"Suck that?" I pointed with a look of disgust.

"Suck my dick," he spoke through clenched teeth.

His sudden reaction made me a bit nervous as he came forward stumbling a bit. He lunged forward in an attempt to grab me but fell on his face. I removed his Rolex from his wrist, the drugs on the table, and his wallet from his pockets. I removed the sticky notepad from my purse.

That ass was amazing! I scribbled on the notepad attaching it to the anal beads before making my exit. I sat slouched down in my Range Rover as I listened to *Young Gunna's* hit *Invest*, allowing the lyrics to invade my mental. I declined Shaniece's call as I tried to stay focus on the task at hand. I'd been parked outside of Esha's place of employment for nearly thirty minutes now, knowing my ex-best friend's schedule like the back of my hand. Shaniece's call would just have to wait. Being that she hit me where it hurt, I figured I'd return the favor and hit her pockets.

I'm just glad I didn't tell her too much of my business. It's only so much she could do with *half the facts*. Dressed in a black and white Adidas tracksuit with no mask. I slowly opened the door and headed in Esha's direction.

I parked just a few cars to the left of her 2016 Impala and watched her strut through the lot with two hefty trash bags in each hand, that put a smile on my face. She was dressed in a pink and blue Puma tracksuit with a pair of cream-colored Ugg boots. She still carried a tremendous amount of sex appeal even without exposing her body. I tiptoed around the older model Honda Accord and crept up behind Esha like a ninja.

"Shit." Esha jumped. "Bitch, you scared me," she confessed placing her hand over her heart.

I remained quiet giving Esha a deadpan expression.

"Fo' real, P, you gon' kill me over some dick?" she said spotting the handgun.

"*Kill you*? If I wanted you dead, I would've been made that happen. I want them bags."

"Or what?" she challenged

"Oh, yeah you testing my gangsta?" I asked looking left then right.

"I'm not just g—"

Before Esha could finish her sentence, I charged her swiftly. The steel connected with her forehead causing her to bleed out instantly

"Help me! Somebody help me!" she yelped.

I continued to bash her face in, with every punch her screams turned into whispers. The thick blood forced a wad of hair to stick to her face. Luckily my outfit was black, so the bloodstains were hardly noticeable.

Whew, I was tired. I looked around cautiously, bent down and snatched up the trash bags. I tossed her Chanel tote over my shoulder, climbed into my truck, and sped off leaving Esha laid out unconscious. I peered over at my phone I glanced at the screen and noticed the unread messages from Shaniece.

//: *Where you at? What's up, chick?*

Merely down the street from my crib, I shot Shaniece a text to let her know I was on my way. I hadn't spoken with her since last night. Esha's hoe ass could be dead for all I care. She's lucky I didn't off her ass. Out of all people, she knew how I felt about Donk. She was there through the good and bad. The tears, fights, gifts, celebrations, etc. Now that I've kicked her ass, I'm pretty sure she would tell Donk about me sleeping around. I'm glad I kept the facts to myself. If the Mollies hadn't fried her brain the dumb bitch would've caught on.

She knew Donk had my heart, he wasn't a random. As I sat in the car dwelling on the what-ifs and the why nots, it only made me want to bust a U-turn and finish Esha's ass. Attempting to block out the nonsense I turned up *Drake and Future's* new hit *Life is Good.*

Minutes later, I pulled into Shaniece's apartment complex leaving Esha's assets behind.

"Where you coming from?" Shaniece asked eyeing me skeptically.

"Handling business, where were your antennas when I was playing in the white boy's shit?"

"I was going to tell you. I saw your missed calls. I was Facetiming Twan. He was rambling off everything I needed to hear at the time."

"So, it's a go?"

"Nah, I need a little more, just one date."

"Okay, bet. Here's a little something to buy yourself something nice to step out in on your date," I offered, handing Shaniece three hundred dollars.

"Damn, you a real bitch P, I appreciate ya'."

"It's all good, baby, I'll see you tomorrow."

Ah'Million

Chapter 10

Arianna

"Where the fuck is Kadejah?" I mumbled looking down at the screen on my phone. Business at the coffee shop was normal it was just boring as hell today with Kadejah and P.J. being absent. When I spoke with Kadejah earlier, she was with Persuasia. It was now an hour till closing, and I couldn't wait.

"I'm about to go on break. You good?" Amy asked.

"Yeah," I responded as I shrugged my shoulders.

"Cool, I'll see you in twenty." She chucked the deuce.

"It's actually fifteen, but okay see you then," I responded dryly.

I didn't care if she was gone an hour, hell Dan could go too. I lazily leaned over the countertop while scrolling down the news feed on my Instagram account. It was the same shit, bitches stunting with they're income tax money, thirsty dudes, side bitches being messy, niggas in the spot, knowing damn well they just the worker yet they stunting with the profit knowing boss man on his way to scoop up his earnings. I deeply exhaled turning my phone over.

Ding! I looked up at the guy coming through the door, but for some odd reason when I tried looking away I couldn't. I mean he was handsome, but it wasn't nothing major. Maybe it was his swag or cocky demeanor. I shoved my phone in my pocket as he approached the counter.

"How you doing? Can I get a large black coffee with a spoon of sugar?"

"No creamer or cappuccino?"

"Nothing mama," he replied placing the five-dollar bill on the counter.

"Oh, and, let me get two of your banana nut muffins with a thin slice of butter on top please."

"Coming right up."

"Dan?" I shouted looking around the back where the kitchen area and office were at.

Dumbfounded I continued to look around the spacious and obvious empty space, there was no Dan. I took two of the fresh muffins off the pan and stuck them in the microwave for twenty seconds carefully placing the thin slice of butter on top. It took less than two minutes to make the black coffee.

"Here you go," I said placing his order in front of him. I almost got lost in his honey-colored eyes, they were mesmerizing.

"Thank you," he responded taking a sip of his coffee.

"Aahhh, just how I like it." He smacked his lips and peered up at me blankly and with that, I walked off.

I turned the volume up on the radio inside the shop and let *Megan Thee Stallion's* hit *Bitch* blast through the speakers.

"Ooohhh, this my shit," I sang along snapping my fingers and moving my hips to the beat while I walked around with the towel, wiping down the tables and windows.

"Hey, can I ask you something?" he yelled from his table.

"Yes," I replied inching closer.

"You got a dude?"

"No." I grinned bashfully feeling a bit shy. I covered the huge grin on my face with the palm of my hand.

"Oh, you want one?" he asked peering up at me while biting into his muffin.

"I don't know." I couldn't stop blushing I hated that I was so light I just knew my entire face was red.

"You don't know? You want me to help you?" he asked looking up at me with those enchanting eyes. He spoke very calmly but with authority.

I hung onto each word like a dying man holding on for dear life. His goatee was trimmed neatly around his juicy lips and his teeth were white as milk.

"How will you do that?" I asked placing my hands on my hip.

"Sit down."

Enthused by his blunt gesture, I swiftly scooted onto the cushioned seat. We talked and laughed. He was extremely funny when he tried to be, and he even had a hilariously dry sense of humor. I could tell he was older, but I didn't ask. I was more afraid of him asking me and once he finds out I'm not even seventeen he'll cut me loose. I sensed he was a bit overprotective which instantly aroused me.

"What's up, y'all?" Amy said coming through the door, walking towards our table.

Seeing her face messed up my entire mood, and from the look on his face, my mood wasn't the only mood she spoiled.

"Excuse me maa—"

"Amy," she intervened holding her hand out.

"I didn't ask your name. If it's okay with you, I'd like to finish my conversation with this beautiful lady in private," he stated leaving Amy looking dumbfounded with her hand still outstretched.

"Oh, okay, excuse me," she said turning around.

"You never told me your name beautiful."

"Arianna and yours?"

"Quincy," he responded glancing back at Amy with a hint of irritation in his eyes.

"What's wrong?"

"Nothing."

"Be for real."

"Ol' girl she just annoying, every time I come up here, she's sweating me and constantly low-key checking for a nigga. Then for her to come over here trying to formally introduce herself like I'm a total stranger to her. She's not your friend with that slick shit knowing she wants to eat my dick."

I covered my mouth at the vulgar language, but oddly it turned me on.

"Well, I didn't expect you to say that."

"Anybody like that is a snake and you don't need to surround yourself around those kinds of people."

I nodded my head while soaking everything in. *How was I going to cut her off and we're coworkers?* I thought.

"What time you get off?"

"At five p.m."

"Okay, if you're cool with it, I'd like to take you out tonight."

"Okay, where are we going?"

"You ask a lot of questions. Just ride this wave, hit me up when you get home," he said sliding his number across the table, written on a piece of napkin.

"Okay," I agreed peering at him.

He possessed a nice, strong build, broad shoulders, 6'2, 250 pounds and his walk was distinctive and sexy.

As I was prepping for my date with Quincy, I sang along to *Chris Brown's – No Guidance,* while I flat ironed my curly hair a few strands at a time. I wanted to look perfect for my date, since leaving the coffee shop, I'd been anticipating seeing him again. I wanted to say something to Amy, but I nutted up. Unlike Kadejah I'm not about that life. I just hope she falls back once I tell her he's mine. Whenever it happens.

"Shit!" I jumped placing the flat irons down. Using my hand to fan my ear. I pushed my hair back noticing the small burn. *Fuck, I done burnt my ear,* I thought.

I didn't have time to dwell on it, I was pissed but I kept going I still hadn't talked to Kadejah I wish she would get here soon so she could help me pick out the perfect outfit. Despite the sound being faint I jerked my head in the direction of my window.

Tap!

There it was again. I placed the flat irons down and crept over to my window. I peeped out my blinds and spotted P.J. leaning against the tree. I wanted to yell I was so excited to see him.

Let me in. He signed with his hands. Sign language was something P.J. and I learned together when I was mentally disoriented and couldn't talk.

I quickly yanked the string down lifting the blinds and unlocked the window sliding it up as far as it could go. P.J. jogged from behind the tree quickly climbing into the window.

"Donk here?" he asked looking around nervously.

"Yeah, last time I checked. What's wrong you good?" I asked a bit concerned.

From a distance, P.J. looked normal. He was dressed in Polo from his shirt, down to his socks. I was sure he'd had a fresh cut, but I couldn't see it due to the matching Polo beanie he rocked. You would've thought his eyelids weighed a ton by how low they were. The effect the Kush had on his outer appearance made my clit thump. I don't know why I was so attracted to this boy.

"I'm good, just a bit edgy now that I know Donk is here. I didn't see his G wagon, so I thought I was good."

"You still good. I'll hide you, sneak you out, or whatever else I have to do."

P.J. flashed a weak smile and pulled his hoodie over his head. A little discomfort came over me, cause the last thing I wanted was P.J. to get comfortable.

"Arianna!" The sound of Donk's voice scared both of us.

"Get in the closet while I go see what he wants," I suggested waiting to open the door to my room.

P.J. grabbed his hoodie and ran inside my closet. I snatched the door open and moved swiftly down the hallway.

"Yes," I answered innocently.

"You got plans for the night?" he asked eyeing me from head to toe.

"Yes, sir. Kianna and I are going to the movies," I quickly lied.

"Look I'm about to dip out I'll be back later. All I'm gon' say is, you better beat me home," he confirmed seriously.

"Okay, see you, Unc," I said running down the hallway to finish getting dressed.

"I'm leaving your money on the table!" he shouted.

I closed the door to my room and quickly ran to my closet. P.J. was knocked out leaning against my pile of dirty laundry. He must have been tired. I let him sleep while I begin to get dressed. I finish straightening the last section of my hair. The lights on my vanity made it easy for me to see the smallest pimple.

I applied a little foundation, just enough to cover a few dark spots. The Youtube tutorial taught me how to do my brows, with all the practice I'd become a beast. I skipped the eyeshadow and applied a little mascara to my individuals I had done by the chinks at the nail shop earlier this week. I placed my MAC snob lipstick on the table so I could apply a few coats before heading out. Moving around a sleeping P.J. I grabbed my wool Micheal Kors long sleeve,

V-neck, black MK skinny jeans, and my grey, thigh-high boots I bought from Aldo's to match the sweater.

I would definitely have to beat Uncle Donk home dressed like this but I was adamant on impressing Quincy. I heard the front door slam and the sound of Uncle Donk's car alarm. I ran and peered out the window to see if he was leaving, sure enough, he was.

Bing! I unlocked my phone and read the message from the unknown number.

Unknown: //: Hey this Quincy, send me your address I'm gon' pull up on you in 30 minutes.

I jumped up and down like a kid on Christmas day.

Me: //: 5628 Black Jack Oaks Dr. 75227

I tossed my phone on the bed while stripping down to my underclothes. I quickly but thoroughly lotioned my body down.

"Where you going? P.J. asked stepping out of the closet.

"I'm going on a date, P.J."

"*A date?* Why you just now telling me you made plans?"

"You not my dude, I didn't think I had to. You never tell me any of your business."

"Oh, yeah? You saying that to say what?"

"Nothing, I'm just stating facts. Donk gone," I continued, pulling my sweater over my head. I stood back on my legs, poking my chest out a little more seeing that P.J. was eyeing me like a caged lion.

"I bet that nigga lame."

"Don't worry 'bout that. Are you going to crash here or what?"

"So, you really gon' leave and I'm here Ari?" I could see the sadness in his eyes, but I wanted to have fun and maybe wild out a bit and with P.J. that wasn't guaranteed.

"Yeah, I'm going to go P.J."

"Man, that's fucked up I haven't seen you in like three days, bruh. Where is my sister at?"

"That's what I was about to ask you."

Suddenly, my phone rang and Quincy's number flashed across the screen.

"I'll see you later," I said to P.J. and headed out of the house, abruptly. I could tell from the wrinkles in his forehead that he was upset, but he didn't voice it.

"So, I hope I didn't overdress," I said while putting my seat belt on. It was cold as hell outside and Quincy's white Range Rover felt warm and cozy.

"Just a little," Quincy shot back, he was sitting next to me looking delicious, but I wasn't going to tell him that.

P.J. was upset about me leaving but a girl's got to do what a girl's got to do. He promised to be in my closet when I return, but I don't believe it he never sat still for too long. I hope he is. *Tank - When We* played softly as I stared out the window. I'm hoping for a nice restaurant, but the movies is cool, too. I still haven't made time to see the movie *Hustlers* with *Cardi B* and *J-Lo*.

"Why you so quiet?" Quincy asked.

He wore an all-red Supreme tracksuit with a pair of white and gold hi-top Lebron's. Every now and then he would brush his hand across his waves. I thought the gesture was sexy.

"Oh, I didn't realize I was quiet. May I ask where we going?"

"Why does it matter?" he retorted surprising me a bit.

"Oh, I was just asking," I quickly responded turning away from his glare.

We pulled into these apartments and he swerved to the side and typed the code in. The gates opened and he zoomed inside. The apartments were nice, there were a few people scattered around the pool. We bypassed the pool and first section of the apartments, swerving around the corner. He parked in the next section and killed the engine.

"Come on," he said immediately climbing out.

I followed suit I couldn't believe I got all dolled up to come to this guy's house. Pissed wasn't even the word. I followed behind Quincy taking the steps two at a time, crossing my arms over my breasts while he unlocked the door. His apartment had a feminine touch, but I wasn't going to comment. The mahogany sectional was decorated with Khaki and black pillows.

"Get comfortable, ma," he said dropping his keys on the table.

Get comfortable is the last thing I want to do, I thought. I wanted to remove my boots but decided against it.

"So, today we gon' Netflix and chill!" Quincy yelled from the kitchen. "I'm going to cook us up a meal with a nice dessert," he continued.

A smile spread across my face and suddenly things didn't seem so bad. "Okay," I said sitting down on the sectional. I looked down at my lit screen spotting the message alert.

Unknown: //: Bruh, I'm bout' 2 go. Holla at U tomorrow.

Me: //: Who this

Unknown: //: P.J. my bad I forgot to tell you I lost my phone last night, this my new number.

Me: //: Okay. You're not still mad R you?

Unknown: //: Hell yeah, I see where ya loyalty lies. Kadejah would've done no shit like this.

I didn't even respond. I placed the phone inside my pocket and flipped through the channels. An hour later shrimp and fettuccini pasta, garlic toast, green beans, and sweet corn covered the plate Quincy placed in front of me.

"Ooohhh, this looks good," I praised as I picked up my fork and dug in.

"Before you put that fork in your mouth, remove your jacket and say your grace."

Embarrassed, I sat the fork with the noodles wrapped around it down on my plate. Avoiding eye contact I looked down at the floor while removing the thin sweater. I stood to lay it over the arm of the couch when Quincy politely took it out of my hand and hung it up. I sat back down placing the napkin across my lap.

"God is good, God is great. Thank you for this food, amen."

"Dear Heavenly Father we come before you thanking you for this food we about to receive and thank you for the hands that prepared it and the hands who served it. In your most precious name, Amen."

The food is probably cold by now, I thought.

"Let's eat," Quincy spoke up irritating the hell out of me.

My mind was so scattered I hadn't paid any attention to Quincy's appearance. He looked comfortable but sexy in just a tank top and basketball shorts. He peered up at me intensely while eating his food. I wasted no time eating, I just didn't want to upset Quincy. After the delicious meal, Quincy and I laid cuddled up on a blanket by the fireplace in front of the 60-inch flatscreen. Although the T.V. was on we were both caught up in our own conversation. It started funny and harmless, but now the questions had become personal and serious.

"What's your biggest fear?" he asked while rubbing his finger-tips up and down my thigh.

"You," I shot back. I didn't mean to be so honest, but it just rolled off my tongue.

"Oh, yeah?" he asked lifting on his elbows while gazing into my eyes.

"Yes, Quincy."

"How you going to fear someone that cares so much about you?"

"I don't know, it's just the way you make me feel is unreal. The effect you already have on me is dangerous and I—" Before I could finish my sentence, he placed his lips on top of mine and attacked me like a caged animal would do a piece of steak.

His tongue became his weapon as he continued the attack. I kissed him back the best way I knew how. The only time I ever kissed is when I was forced to do so by my dirty foster father.

"Let's fight ya' fears," he stated tugging at my clothes.

I watched him in silence while allowing him to rip my clothes off. I wanted so badly to object, although the attraction was evident. I didn't want to upset him or allow him to think I was lame and begin to doubt my maturity. I figured I'd let him take advantage of me sexually, once he finds out my age it'll already be too late. A look of confusion spread across my face when I saw him untuck my pants from underneath my boots and slide my pants down over my boots.

The cool breeze caused my nipples to harden and once Quincy noticed he dove in, caressing and sucking my breasts. I closed my eyes and prepared for a night to remember. As he was positioned on top of me I spread my legs further as an unspoken invitation. The feel of his weight against my small frame made me anxious for what was next to come. He slid his hand down to my treasure box and begin massaging my clit with his middle finger.

"Ooohhh, that feels good Quincy," I voiced biting down on my lip.

Using one arm to position himself on his elbow he used the other to pull down his basketball shorts and briefs. I learned in school that no protection isn't safe, but I didn't care. I just wanted to satisfy and be satisfied. He slid his finger up and down my wet opening and stuck his finger in his mouth.

"You taste good, too," he whispered while rubbing his thick tip against my kitty.

I looked down at his massive dick and my eyes grew twice the size at the sight. I gasped for air as he entered me. I dug my freshly manicured nails into his back as he eased himself inside of me an inch at a time.

"Ooohhh, it's too big Quincy. Please stop bae," I begged.

A wicked smile spread across his face and I could tell he enjoyed my cries. I bit down on my lip as I tried to endure the pain, but it was no use. He forcefully thrust the last inch or two inside me causing me to yelp out in pain while he slowly dug in and around my walls, like someone's foot caught in quicksand, who is trying to escape resembled Quincy's movement inside my pussy. A few more strokes and my little love box loosened turning the pain into pleasure. The left stroke was the best stroke. If he continued to hit me like this, I think I might have a stroke.

"Ooohhh, yes, fuck me, Quincy! This your pussy," I said swiping away the loose strands of hair that were sticking to my face.

"Oh, yeah, it's mine? Show me it's mine. Cum for me," he said putting my legs behind my head.

I thought the position would be uncomfortable, but it actually drove me nuts cause it enabled him to hit my spot with each thrust. I never felt a feeling so amazing before in my life. My eyes rolled to the back of my head, and my body went limp as if someone had just sucked all the bones out of my body. I begin to shake uncontrollably, and I felt an eerie feeling about to happen that was unfamiliar.

"Cum for me, bae," Quincy whispered.

My moans grew louder as his pace quickened. I thought I would pass out from all the pleasure.

"Aaaagghhhh!" I yelled out as the warm liquid shot out of my pussy and landed on the coffee table behind us.

"What was that?" I asked in total shock, lifting up on my elbows.

"You never squirted before?" he asked.

"No, I haven't."

"It's okay, bae only a nigga like me can make you do things like that. Take those boots off and come lay down."

Ah'Million

Chapter 11

Kadejah

Donk would definitely kick my ass right now if he knew I was in the car with these strangers. Young or old they were all the same. I tried to relax while listening to the *Kodak Black's* lyrics, but I just couldn't for some odd reason.

"You smoke?" Nando asked, peering at me in the rearview mirror.

"No," I lied, fixing my face into a frown. The only person I did smoke with from time to time was P.J. Donk always said if I smoked, roll my own shit cause a nigga will lace the weed whatever that meant.

"Come on ma let loose, I'm not gon' bite you." He smiled.

"I'm good," I repeated firmly.

He shrugged his shoulders and turned back around. I wasn't really nervous cause I had texted P.J. whatever information Uncle Mun, Donk, and the cops needed, just in case.

"Hey, you missed your turn," I voiced calmly.

"What?" he answered peering at me through the rearview mirror

"You missed the turn."

"Okay, so what you going with me. We just gon' chill, calm down."

"Hell nah! What you mean calm down? I don't know you!"

"Javier," he voiced calmly.

In a flash, the boy on the passenger side turned around and pressed the burner against my temple.

"Give me your phone," he requested holding his hand out.

I quickly handed my phone over. I wanted to slap myself, hopping in the car with these Mexicans was the dumbest decision I ever made. I didn't even know these dudes. Fucking with Tru really had my mind gone, I'd been taking a risk without considering the consequences.

If my black ass ends up dead, Uncle Donk will have no under-standing, I thought.

The gunman turned back around once he had possession of my phone. I discreetly grabbed the door handle but as I yanked on it, I realized it was locked. I looked to the side and behind me franti-cally. The car began to slow down making me nervous and I did something I should've done a long time ago, I shot a quick prayer to the man that created the Heavens and Earth. The car came to a complete stop then Nando killed the engine, Javier hopped out first. We were parked in front of a typical modest home something that may have belonged to his parents although I had an eerie feeling they weren't home.

"Get out!" Javier demanded as he opened my door.

Once Fernando hopped out, he stood behind Javier as if he'd need help for little ol' me.

Someone is inside. I thought.

As I spotted the blinds inside the house move. I was nervous at first, but now I was so terrified I was shaking like a stripper barely able to walk. Javier gripped my arm tighter with every step.

"Quit playing and walk right before I make my goon whack yo' ass right here," he threatened.

I lifted my leg to climb the steps to the porch when the sound of screeching tires caught my attention.

Ssskkkrrr!

"What the fuck?" I spoke in disbelief with my mouth flung open.

"Hey, Gon' *un-ass* her before I call my back up!" Mr. Woods yelled walking up the front yard.

He flashed some type of badge as well as the symbol on his collared shirt. Javier looked at Fernando unsure of what to do next. They must've thought Mr. Woods was a real policeman.

"Thanks, officer," I added being extra.

"Let her go," Nando whispered trying to appear unbothered.

Javier loosened his death grip and I ran into the arms of Mr. Woods. We wasted no time getting to the car. I was so relieved I wanted to dive in face first. Mr. Woods took off like a Nascar driver, he looked pretty shook as well.

"Man, if them niggas would've called my bluff, me and you would probably be dead, right now," he said tossing the badge out the window.

"Hey, your badge!" I yelled looking out the back window.

"That's fake, it was part of my uniform for Halloween. I was a cop."

I burst out laughing unable to control it. "Damn you saved my life. How did you even know?"

"Well, when I went out to my car on my lunch break, I saw the truck lingering by the bus stop. So, when I pulled up behind it, I saw you climbing in and I could tell by your hesitation that you didn't know them. So, I followed you."

"I'm glad you did."

"Yeah, I'm glad I did, too," Mr. Woods said peering into my eyes.

We came to a stop at the red light and he removed his uniform shirt. His muscles peeked through his tank top and I looked away before I began to drool.

"So, can I have an hour of your time?" he asked gazing into my eyes

"You just save my life you can have two hours," I joked.

"I'm gon' hold you to that, my two don't start until we get to my place."

"Cool."

"Here take my coat," Mr. Woods suggested throwing the massive North Face coat over my shoulders while we walked up the walkway leading to the two-story house.

I kept licking my lips to prevent them from chapping, but it was no use. He quickly unlocked the door and I flew past him inside. The house was warm and cozy, it sort of resembled your grandmother's house with merely a hint of masculinity. Different pictures of imperative past events decorated the wall. Men like Martin Luther King, Malcolm X, and Blues singer B.B. King. Along with beautiful women of color, Maya Angelou and Rosa Parks. The sofa, lamps tables, and any other miscellaneous decorations were black.

"Let me get that for you," he offered removing his coat and my thin hoodie.

He held them in one hand and with his other hand, he grasped my hand and led me to the sofa. As soon as my ass hit the cushion, he kneeled to remove my shoes.

"Mr. W—"

"Quit calling me that, my name is Caleb."

"Oh, so, Caleb Woods we're on first-name basis now?"

"I just prefer Caleb, ma."

"Okay, that's cool. Oh, and your two hours started when you removed my coat."

He laughed while walking to the back of the house. I looked around patiently while twinkling my toes.

"Hey, I'm not much of a cook. So, just tell me what you have in mind and I'll order it."

"Chinese Food."

"Oh, we got something in common that's my favorite. Do you mind if I order for you?"

"Yes, I'm sort of picky. I want Sesame chicken, Orange chicken, and a small Shrimp fried rice with two egg rolls."

"Okay, I'll get the same thing." Caleb walked towards the back and ordered the food.

I made a mental note to buy a new phone since my attackers took my last one. I couldn't wait to tell Uncle Donk what had occurred. Tru had been on my mind heavy and I wanted to see her home more than anything if she thought for one second that the time and distance would separate us she thought wrong. A visit, letter, cash? How simple is that? Being that I love her I'm willing to do a lot more than that and no one is gon' stop me.

"Okay, they'll be here in ten minutes," he announced sitting down on the sofa beside me

"Netflix?" he asked. I shrugged my shoulders in response. "What's wrong?" he continued.

"Nothing," I said looking down at my hands.

"You still afraid from what happened earlier?"

"Nah, once I tell my Uncles it'll be taken care of."

"Then what's wrong?"

"I really miss Oshae," I confessed as the tears fell from my eyes.

"I don't mean to dirty mack, Kadejah. But do you know how much time that girl has?"

"Huh, *how much*?" I asked dumbfounded through sniffles. "What do you mean? She's coming home any day now," I continued peering up into his eyes as if I was searching for something.

"No, Kadejah, she has a life sentence."

"You're lying," I gasped. "Tru would've told me that! Why you making shit up?" I asked full of rage standing to my feet.

"Lie for what? Calm down shorty she must've lied to you. I'm not going to lie to you. I'm all for what makes you happy."

How you all for my happiness when you barely even know me? I thought. "She wouldn't lie to me."

Caleb hopped to his feet and grabbed his laptop off the dining room table. "I'll just show you since you don't believe me." My heart was beating so fast I could hear it and it was fucking up my concentration. "What's her first name?"

"Lytrice."

"See?" he said handing me the laptop.

I looked at the screen in disbelief, wide-eyed and speechless. I just couldn't believe the information displayed before me. "A murder charge?" I voiced aloud to no one in particular.

I looked over at Caleb for reassurance, to tell me anything other than what I was seeing. He sat there peering straight ahead while stroking his goatee. Tears fell constantly as I slowly passed Caleb the laptop.

Life, really? I thought.

"They talked about her like she's some monster," I whispered looking up at him.

"I don't know what to say, ma."

"She's not a monster, Caleb."

"You saying that like you've known this girl. You knew her for three weeks!"

"So, what! I know her and I love her and I'm going to help her!"

"Okay, whatever you want to do. We'll help her together."

Bing!

He jogged to the door and retrieved the food. It smelled delicious, but I was too upset to eat.

"Come on girl and eat, what's done is done."

"You right, all I can do is be there for her."

"For life?" he asked peering up into my eyes.

"Yes, until the day I go. Love and loyalty have no expiration date. I'm not going to leave her high and dry for making a mistake. She committed a crime and the judge mercilessly sentenced her. I'm going to see if I can get a lawyer to look for any loopholes. Would you want someone to give up on you?"

Caleb didn't respond he just peered at me silently. I grabbed my fork and picked at my food while I thought of different ways I could help Tru. Caleb remained surprisingly quiet. I leaned over and rested my head on his lap. I lost interest in the movie a long time ago. I was exhausted and my mind was all over the place.

"In the morning can you take me to get a phone?"

"No problem, I'll pay for it, too."

This nigga is really trying to bag a bitch, I thought.

"I'm okay I have money. Let me see your laptop to check my Facebook to see if my uncle has an APB out for me," I joked.

As he logged on Caleb leaned over and planted soft wet kisses from my collar bone past my arm down to my hand. It was a bit sudden, but it felt so inviting. I had a few unread messages from Lil Tim, but that was it.

Lil Tim: //: Where you at lil' baby I need you. I'll send Uber if need be just let me know where you at.

I scrolled down and opened the next one.

Lil Tim: //: They released me from the hospital, and I need a little help around the house. Peaches somewhere with the next nigga.

What's the address here?" I asked Caleb catching him off guard

"Why, Kadejah?"

"My cousin just got out of the hospital and he's not at his best. He needs me."

"So, its fuck me, huh?" he protested smacking his lips.

"What's the address," I repeated

"One-eight-two-nine Big Stone Gap Road, Duncanville, Texas, seven-five-one-three-seven."

"Thank you." I typed the address in quickly and in a matter of seconds, Lil Tim messaged back, informing me the Uber would arrive shortly. Caleb sat on the side of me with his lips poked out evidently upset.

"Caleb," I softly spoke. "Caleb!" I repeated, yet no response. I nudged his arm forcing him to look my way. "Don't be mad at me."

"Man, I'm not."

"Yes, you are," I replied standing to my feet then straddling him.

Appalled at my boldness, he peered at me seriously. I wanted so badly to read his mind, but I didn't have to once I felt his massive hands squeeze my ass. He used his nose to lift my chin as he began sucking softly on my neck. I didn't want to go there but I wasn't going to stop him.

"You gon' be mine, Kadejah?" he asked in between soft kisses. His lips felt like clouds and my young and inexperienced ass was satisfied enough with his lips alone. I closed my eyes while enjoying the satisfaction.

Honk! Honk!

"I have your card in my pocket. I'll give you a call as soon as I buy a phone. See you later," I said gathering my things.

Caleb opened his mouth to say something, but I silenced him with a kiss before flying out the door.

Ah'Million

Chapter 12

P.J.

I mobbed down the busy street end route to Bubba's house. Trigga wasn't answering for whatever reason and I just really wasn't feeling Bando. Lately, he'd responded nonchalantly to everything expressing this cocky demeanor as if I was beneath him when he was juggin' just like I was. Honestly, since I pulled the strap out on Donk I've been feeling lonely. No Donk meant no Kadejah, despite us talking every day. It still wasn't enough for me. I clutched the small pistol that rested in the pocket of my hoodie and quickened my pace. A drop of rain landed on my nose and I slung the hood on top of my head. I was starting to see Persuasia for who she truly is. My grandma, Lord rest her soul, for years she tried to tell me how foul my mother was, but I wasn't trying to listen. I know blood is thicker than mud, but the ones related to us is not by choice. So, to actually find someone more genuine and loyal than your own family you have to keep them around.

Since climbing out of Arianna's window I'd been trying to reach Donk, but I continue to get the voicemail. I was merely five minutes away from Bubba's house but decided to veer off inside the 7-eleven. The Hispanic chick at the register eyed me lustfully. I removed my hood and made my way through the spacious store. Everyone seemed to get quiet once I entered. The mumbling and laughing ceased, the only thing I could hear was the squeaking from my shoes. I picked up a bag of hot fries for Bubba and a bag of hot Cheetos for myself.

I walked to the next aisle where the chili and cheese machine was located. A group of dudes stood in the corner talking close to a whisper. Whatever they were discussing it had to be important, because of the way their eyes roamed as they spoke. They weren't just anybody and I could tell that by the way, they were drippin'.

I'm 'bout to get these niggas, I thought as I pulled out my phone to dial Bubba's number.

I propped the phone on my shoulder and clocked my head to the side balancing the phone against my ear while pulling down the handle on the cheese.

"Excuse me, you think you can give us a lift to the nearest rent a car?" the guy dressed in the Dior two-piece asked as he approached me.

I removed the phone from my ear without waiting on Bubba to answer. "I don't got a—hold on," I paused holding up my index finger as I accepted Bubba's call.

"What up, boy," Bubba spoke loudly into the receiver.

"I'm down the street at the seven-eleven, you want something?"

"Nah, I'm good. Trigga say do you want him to come scoop you? He just pulled up."

"Hell yeah, it's raining."

"Bet."

I ended the call and diverted my attention to the guy who stood in front of me.

"Look my name's, Rah Tobias, I'm a music producer. I got my upcoming artist and two of my men from the sound crew with me. We from Atlanta just left a show in New Orleans and drove through Texas. We just trying to get back to the A," he explained.

I looked at him than the men that stood behind him. "Music producer, huh?" I asked rubbing my invisible goatee.

"Yes, I'm one of the best. I have a few connects in high places my brother."

I thought about Bubba while the dude rambled on and on about his accomplishments. Bubba had been looking high and low for his big break, but nothing was working. I know my boy is talented. We spent so many nights, cold nights to be exact on the block, in the alley, porch wherever Kush in the air listening to Bubba flow off the dome. Just the two of us, I remember the long days out on the pavement. Starting fires with trash that lingered the sidewalks, chip bags, old newspaper articles, and whatever else to keep the fire going just so we could withstand the cool temp. For a little while longer. I'd do anything to see my dawg make it.

"Check this, my big homie at my spot. He'll give you a ride, but I have this one request," I voiced

"What's that? We got bread."

"Nah, my bro got bars. I'm talking 'bout some shit that'll make you stop the beat on his ass. You think you can put him on the map?"

"If he's as live as you say he is, then, hell yeah! Let's go, I'm anxious to hear the kid."

On cue, I spotted Trigg's truck swerve into the empty parking space.

"Come on, team," Rah called out to his men who stood off to the side.

I paid for my items at the counter and headed outside. I could see the look of confusion on Trigga's face when he realized the men were walking with me. Instead of hopping in, I walked to his side of the truck.

"Aye, I told dude we'll give him and his people a ride to rent a car if he hears Bubba spit. He's a music producer," I stated munching on my hot Cheetos sucking the warm and spicy cheese off my finger.

"Okay, that's a bet. Hop in, hell yeah!" Trigga agreed ecstatically after sizing the men up.

I knew he was thinking like I was thinking, but I strongly felt he'd give Bubba a shot once he heard him.

"Took y'all niggas long enough. Who this?" Bubba asked looking past me.

"This your one shot nigga," I said bypassing a dumbfounded Bubba.

"My one shot?" he repeated following behind me.

"Yeah, ask him what I mean." I nodded my head in Rah's direction.

Bubba turned around and peered at Rah through narrow slits

"I'm Rah Tobias, I'm a—"

"Music producer from ATL?" Bubba interjected.

Rah smiled confidently at Bubba's statement. He looked at Rah in disbelief while Rah silently praised himself as if he was some sort of God.

"Fam, P.J., you know what this shit means? I got Rah Tobias in my crib and B. Gulley with him! Trigga Black, you see this shit man?" he yelled out.

I'd never heard of B. Gulley, but I guess when you're in the game you know it.

"Aye, I told you nigga, you were on your way," I cheered punching the air with my fist, while the flamin' hots was in my other hand.

Rah stuck his hands in his pocket and smirked at Bubba.

"B, show this nigga what you got so y'all can chop it up 'bout ya future and we can get them taken care of. Their car broke down and they need a ride to rent a car. That's when I made him a deal he couldn't refuse."

"Bet, let me grab my CD with a few beats on it," Bubba stated running to his room. I was so happy for Bubba I couldn't sit still.

"Alright, these ain't no top of the line beats, but they mine. I'm gon' flow off the dome, give me a topic."

"Bitches," Rah responded taking a seat on the couch.

"Hand me that Styrofoam off the table big bro'," Bubba asked Trigga who quickly retrieved the cup. He quickly took a sip of the mud and placed it on the table.

"Xans on deck, with a knot in my pocket
I'm full of that Kush, left hand on the rocket
It's time to take off, you pussies can't stop me
Swag impeccable, you know they gon' joc me
The hoes gon' flock me, they sloppily top me.
Dro on deck so I burn it up
I count it up, count it up, count it up
My niggas savages where da money truck?
Money long, put ya wallet up
Move ya glass, we using double cups
I like the purple shit, with a freaky bitch
She gives me top and bottom, back seat and shit
I like em' top dollar, no ratchet shit
My ho' turn thotty, I'ma pass the bitch

Unass the bitch, buckle my seat belt zoom past the bitch!"

"That's enough, that's enough! I like you kid." Rah smiled rubbing his hands together.

"Nigga you was on that hoe!" I yelled walking up and slapping palms with Bubba.

Trigga followed suit and did the same.

"If you doing that off the dome. I know you the truth when your pen starts flowing," B. Gulley chimed in.

Bubba stood there nodding his head accepting the praise. The sound crewmen even showed love.

'Hey, I'm gon' hit you up bright and early in the morning. We have some things we need to discuss, put your name and number in here. Bubba, right?"

This shit is a dream, I thought.

"Yeah, it's Bubba," he answered putting his number in the phone.

"You ready?" Trigga asked fiddling around his pockets for his keys while smiling.

"Yeah, we ready," Rah said looking around at his men as they made their way to the door.

"Bubba, hey, be ready cause I'm going to hit you up soon as I open my eyes," Rah assured backpedaling out the front door.

I hoped Rah wasn't with no bullshit cuz if he was I was going to hunt and gun him down myself.

"You want us to ride, Fam?" I hollered at Trigga.

"Y'all good roll that gas up, I'll be back," he said opening the door.

"These my hot fries?" Bubba asked closing the door. "Man, Fam, I 'preciate you for that shit for real, you don't know how big this is."

"You good, I know how much music means to you. I just hope Rah is a man of his word."

"He will or we will if everything goes as planned the jug and finesse season is over!"

"What you mean we will. What you do?" I chuckled."

"Member those little tracking devices I bought offline the other day?"

"Yeah."

"I slipped one into his jacket when I dapped him up."

"You a fool."

Last night turned into a celebration, Bubba's mother's house was so smoked out, here it was hours later and I could barely see cause of the smoke. I knew she'd be home in an hour or so, so I forced myself to get up and air this bitch out before she arrived. I looked down at my Gucci bracelet watch, seeing that it was 5:49. I didn't have long, swisher sweet paper and cigarillo guts decorated the floor. Bubba laid sprawled out on the floor next to the dining table while Trigga laid on the couch. I opened the side door to let a little breeze come in. It was cold as shit, but oh well. I found a blunt as long as my pinky in the ashtray. I put fire to it and puffed on the exquisite weed slowly, as I moved through the front room picking up dirty dishes glass dishes and plastic ones, straightening up the pillows on the couch. I did my best fixing it around Trigga's thin but muscular body. I swept instead of vacuuming, so I wouldn't awake them. I washed the few dishes, emptied the ashtrays, and sprayed a little Lysol before closing the side door. I turned the ceiling fan on and laid back down on the floor, a few inches away from Bubba.

"Y'all asses tired cuz' you been out hoeing all night. Wake up! Sleep all day at ya' own shit. Not my shit!" Ms. V. yelled.

I knew she would do exactly that, that's why I woke up and cleaned up before she got here to keep her nagging at a minimum.

"P.J. and Bubba y'all too young to be so tired?" she continued.

I didn't know sleep had an age requirement, I thought.

Bubba jumped up like he had seen a ghost looking around frantically, while Trigga rose up slowly as if this was a routine. Ms. V was the type to pick, she would find something to fuss about. I could just only imagine her reaction if I would've never cleaned up. She dropped her keys on the table and vanished towards the rear of the house.

"How it get so clean?" Bubba asked half asleep.

"I woke up about an hour and a half ago, cleaned up, and laid back down."

"Damn, bruh, you always looking out. 'Preciate ya' if she would've come home and saw that mess, I probably got kicked out, both of us."

Since the altercation with Donk at the club, I'd been crashing at Bubba's spot. I didn't like being at home with Persuasia transitioning from a boy to a man, there were certain things I just couldn't witness. Doing so would cause detriment and before I found myself in trouble, I'd rather keep my distance. The love I had for her was so profound it was unreal. I also admired and treasured Donk more than anything for stepping up and being the father figure in my life. I never remember a time when I was younger without my dad because Donk was always around holding it down.

Once I was old enough to understand, that's when my mother told me the truth about Donk not being my real father. It was confusing and bothered me deeply. I didn't begin to understand until years later as I got of age. It didn't bother me as much then because he still treated me like his. That's why I made up my mind after today I would put my pride to the side and makeup with Donk. Life's too short to dwell on other's faults.

"Hey, y'all want to hit somethin'? This lil' broad I fuck with just texted me and told me she saw the people down the street leave. I been scoping this house for months, if y'all want to go we have to move now," Trigga said sitting on the edge of the sofa.

"It don't matter to me. Rah, supposed to call and invite Bubba to his studio today," I explained.

"Let's go chase this sack. The quicker we leave, the quicker we'll make it back and be ready for Rah's call," Bubba chimed in.

"Y'all with it, I'm with it."

Dressed in yesterday's clothes we climbed into Trigga's Yukon. I sat in the backseat in silence as I thought of ways to approach Donk. This lick didn't break or make me. I had $2,600.00 put up and $300 in my pocket. The fact is, we weren't just partners in crime. Bubba and Trigga were like family and since day one we'd made an unspoken pact and that pact was to ride. Not just ride to accompany one another but to hold it down in whatever form or fashion.

"The house 'bout seven houses down. It's six-eight-five-one alongside the curb. I'm going to park right here. Check this we gon' do this like we always do. We came together, that's how we gon' leave. Ten minutes and we out. If it's something big I'll run and get the whip. Til the ragz," Trigga quoted, turning around in his seat.

"Til the Tagz," Bubba and I responded bumping fists.

We climbed out of the truck and mobbed down the quiet street. It was still early 7:56 a.m. to be exact. My grandmother called these houses egg houses. They were so close together you could toss an egg from one window to the next. Although the houses were so close together the cars parked out front were nice, and I had yet to see any sign of poverty.

Bing!

Bubba quickly removed his phone from his pocket.

"Bruh, this Rah, he gon' come scoop me this afternoon," Bubba spoke full of excitement.

"Hell yeah! You still want to do this or head back?" I said.

"We have time, come on," he said picking up his pace.

I shook my head from left to right in complete disagreement as I followed suit.

"Six-eight-five-one, right here." I pointed to the white and black house. No car was parked out front or the driveway. Bubba you go ring the doorbell, just to make sure.

"I'll check the windows to the left. P.J. you check the ones on the right to see if they're open," Trigga called out walking up the front yard.

I veered off to the side to check the windows. I looked cautiously, while I walked to the window. A few cars had passed, but nothing out of the ordinary. I attempted to slide up the first window, but it was locked so I tried the other one. I grabbed the bottom of the window and slid it up, to my surprise it moved.

Psst! Psst!

I discreetly sounded to get Bubba and Trigga's attention. Trigga gave me the green light, so I slid the window all the way up, lifted my jeans above my belly button, and climbed into the window right leg first. Completely inside, I scanned the darkroom. The light from the window was no help at all- I blindly made my way through the room using the walls for support. I could hear Trigga climbing in as I continued to pat the walls. Nearly bumping into something hard. I stumbled upon a light switch. Quickly flicking it on I spotted an older Hispanic guy sitting in the corner of the room in a wooden chair, holding a twelve-gauge shotgun pointed directly at me.

"Shit!" Frantically I moved as fast as I could to get out the window but Trigga stood behind Bubba who was in the process of climbing out.

"Hurry up Bubba he got a gun! Man, this nigga gon' kill me!" I panicked shoving Trigga in his back so I could make it out, but it was no use.

Boom!

Ah'Million

Chapter 13

Lil' Tim

I'd called Peaches trifling ass for the 99th time and still no answer. I sat on the sofa waiting for Kadejah when I heard the doorbell ring. I lied to Kadejah the hospital didn't actually release me. I got dressed and snuck out, sitting in there was similar to being in jail with better visitation hours and a remote.

"I'm so glad you could make it man. No one wants to answer they're phone for a nigga."

"Fuck them I got you. I wasn't busy or anything, I was just chilling at Persuasia's crib," she lied.

Although I'd been to Persuasia's a few times. I knew it was in Desoto and not Duncanville.

"You hungry?" she asked

"Nah, I ordered McDonald's through Uber eats."

"Oh, okay."

I knew Kadejah had lied to me about her whereabouts, but I was curious to know why. I decided to keep my curiosity to myself. When people lie, I assume it's for a good reason, because that's the type of man I am. However, in a life or death situation, I'm *lying,* hands down.

"So, gon' tell me the juice on Peaches hoe ass."

"She's fuckin' with Melo."

"*Melo?* Jackboy Melo?"

"Yes, Melo's grimy ass. It's a price on his head, right now."

"What's the tag?" I grinned.

"I don't know, but I can find out. You know I hear all the tea at Pig's Beauty Shop."

"Cool, damn I can't even say I'm surprised. I knew what it was when I signed up."

Peaches and I met one day while I was at the spot with Bando. He kept a different bitch in there, a few of them I'd seen periodically. I knew the ones that I'd never see again. Bando just wanted to wam bam, then put them out, but for Peaches, he had a different plan. Not wifey or girlfriend but a position in general. A title that he would keep track of mentally, mindful not to voice it.

You know once a bitch knows she has a label she wants to flex her authority. They can't just chill and be content, they always want more. They want theirs, yours, and your mother shit. So, Bando and I had this indirect test we did. That we've done plenty of times before. It started innocent and unintentional, something we stumbled upon.

Bando, Peaches, and I were chilling, smoking, listening to trap music, and playing the PS4. I respect my homie's main bitches and BMs but anything else is up for grabs.

"Y'all want something from the store?" Bando asked us.

We hollered out a list of things then I took a toke and passed her the blunt.

"Y'all going to see Boosie in concert this weekend?"

"Not if shit jumping around here."

"You d-"

"Look ma, you bad as fuck. I saw you peeping me, let ya boy hit. We both grown, I can keep a secret." Shorty looked at me in shock, surprised by my blunt comment.

"Nah, I'm good," she detested with a hint of hesitation. The hesitation spoke volumes alone.

"What happens with us, is between me and you. That's my boy and all but my business is my business. I don't speak on what I do with my dick." It was as if she was waiting on a little assurance.

She looked out the blinds and quickly begin to undress. In one swift motion, I yanked my jeans and briefs down altogether, within seconds my mans was rock hard. I bent down to remove the condom from my pocket. I let her do the honors by sliding it on. I hit shorty on the edge of the couch, against the door, doggy style then she got on top and rode me like a rollercoaster. Bando pulled up while we were getting dressed. At first Peaches and I was sitting a few inches from each other, but things had become so awkward she was now sitting on the other side of the room. I could sense Bando felt the tension soon as he walked in. It was so thick you could cut it. We made eye contact and he peeped the new seating arrangement his shoulders sort of sagged in defeat.

"You fucked?" he spoke calmly.

"Yeah, boy!" I smirked.

"Damn," Peaches blurted, jerking her neck in my direction. Her gaze was priceless, yet I'd seen it so many times before.

"Get out!" Bando ordered.

"How I'm supposed to get home?"

"You figured out how to fuck. Now figure out how to get home," he said with his back to her.

Me and Peaches' eyes met, and she was no longer in a state of shock she was giving me a death glare, but just like the rest of them. She stomped out slamming the door behind her.

"How long she last?" Bando asked once she left.

"About two minutes. She did tell me no at first."

"Damn, I did like her but fuck that thot." That was the end of Peaches.

Up until I saw her at the Footlocker inside of the Keist Shopping Center a few weeks later. I'm not going to lie she looked stunning, but trashy bitches just isn't that important to me, I don't care how good they look. That day Peaches and I exchanged numbers I held out a few weeks before I let her suck me dry. She put it on me that night, so whenever my mans got hard Peaches was the first chick I called. She even introduced me to a new pill plug with prices lower than fake designer. She let me turn her spot into the pill and chill spot. I never gave Peaches a title. She knew her role and played it well. We been rockin' up until the night I was kidnapped.

"You miss the bitch?" Kadejah asked with her nose flared.

"Nah, calm down killa," I smirked. "I'm going to make us some breakfast," I continued struggling to my feet.

"Sit down! That's why I'm here. Besides I just ate," Kadejah protested pushing me back down on the sofa. "It looks a mess in here and the smell isn't too appeasing either," she said looking around.

"Well, I thought I'd fix you something to eat since you done came all the way over here. The least I could do is treat you. You know I been gon' all this time, this place hasn't been touched. Shit, I'm glad I paid my rent in full."

"When is your lease up?"

"It's just a year, I have six more months."

"Okay, well, we can skip the meal since we've eaten already, Do you need to bathe?"

"Yeah, then I can chill."

"Okay, let me clean this place up, then you can bathe. No telling what it looks like in there," Kadejah said removing her jacket and putting her long bundles in a messy ponytail.

I grabbed the remote off the table, went to Youtube, and scrolled through the Kevin Gates videos while Kadejah cleaned up. She vacuumed, dust, threw the food away in the freezer and refrigerator. She took out the trash, wiped the tables, washed dishes, and scrubbed the bathrooms.

"Whew! I'm tired, Tim," she said crashing backward onto the sofa next to me. Her chest heaved up and down as she removed the strands of hair that was stuck to her sweaty face.

"Prop your legs up here," I said patting my thigh.

One at a time I carefully picked up Kadejah's tiny feet and massaged them. I knew it felt good because she closed her eyes. I was sure she had fallen asleep. I rubbed each foot for an additional ten minutes and placed them back down on my legs. I didn't want to awake her just yet, she looked so peaceful.

"How long was I asleep." She jumped up.

I guess she must've felt me watching her. "Just through the massage, I finished about ten minutes ago."

"Come on, you ready?"

"Yeah." I slowly eased up.

I was fine just really weak. Kadejah grabbed my hand as we walked to the bathroom. My left foot dragged a bit, but other than that I was fine. It smelled fresh and looked spotless.

"Sit right here," she said pulling down the top of the toilet.

She turned the water on and prepped the bathwater while I sat on the toilet.

"I don't want all that fruity shit in there," I protested.

"Be quiet this isn't fruity it's Epsom salt, I got this." She turned off the hot water and began to help me out of my clothes. "Lift your arms." I attempted to lift my arms up high over my head, but it was a bit painful "Oh, okay, just bend a little and stretch out your arms instead."

She said as she removed the tank top. She slightly bent over and pulled down my basketball shorts. I knew my briefs were next which made me feel awkward and uncomfortable. Once my briefs came down, I saw Kadejah's initial reaction before she looked away. I slowly stood to my feet and moved towards the two. I used the wall to balance myself while I stepped inside the tub one leg at a time. The temperature of the water was perfect. I eased down into the water using the sides of the tub to prevent myself from slipping.

"Aahhh," I voiced. A Sharp pain shot through my arms after I released the sides of the tub.

"Damn, you really fucked up? Here give me that," Kadejah said gently grabbing the towel and Irish Spring body wash from my hands. I followed directions as given whether I needed to lift my arms or spread my legs, I tried greatly to do so.

"Whew! This shit's hurting my back," she admitted leaning over the tub with her hands resting on her side. "On the real, it'll be easier if you get in," I suggested, peering into her eyes.

"Get in?" she asked.

"Kadejah take off your clothes and get in this tub. We'll bathe each other."

"You serious?" she asked gawking down at me in awe.

"Don't I look serious?"

Kadejah didn't utter a word, she handed me the towel and body wash and begin removing her clothes.

"You scared?" I asked once she began to slow her pace, the hesitation was evident.

"You saw me strip. What's up?" I continued.

"I got a body like a Benz so ain't no pressure with getting na-ked. I'm just afraid of what might happen next."

"Body like a Benz?" I chuckled. "Yeah, I'll be the judge of that, and you let me worry about what will happen next. Come on," I continued. One leg at a time Kadejah climbed into the tub. "Your shit looks more like a nice Honda. I don't know 'bout no Benz," I joked as Kadejah slapped me on the arm playfully.

Her body was very appeasing. Just a few scars here and there. "Rough childhood don't look at those," she said using her hands to try and cover them all at once.

"Move," I voiced grabbing her hands. "They're not scars, they're beauty marks."

"Come on," she said retrieving the towel and soap from the ledge of the tub. She began to bathe me while I leaned back and watched her closely. In spite of the age difference, I love Kadejah. I'm aware of the crush she has always had on me, being that I was seven years older I had to wait until she was at least old enough to understand. Today, I really had no plans on making my move, but the form of imprisonment I recently endured had my hormones all over the place. Somehow, I allowed my feelings and my dick to speak up. For a long time, I just wanted to love and be loved.

"Your turn," I said grabbing the towel.

"Let me turn around," she suggested placing her back against my chest.

I gently scrubbed her upper chest and stomach. We stayed in the tub until we both were squeaky clean. My mans kept jumping, I know Kadejah felt it on her back. I drained the bathwater then we rinsed off underneath the showerhead. I climbed out of the shower and she used the towel to dry my body. I grabbed her face and pressed her lips into mine. I couldn't contain the urge for another second. The water dripping off her body made it difficult for me to resist. I admired her C cup breasts that sat up like doorknobs. Her stomach was on flat, and her nice bubble butt poked out enhancing her slim physique.

"Gon' go to the front, I'll grab you something to sleep in."

Immediately she spun on her heels and headed to the front. I smirked as I watched her walk away. I grabbed her a shirt and myself a pair of briefs and eased back down the hall. Once I entered the living room, I noticed Kadejah had made a pallet on the floor out of blankets. She laid on her stomach with her legs up. I dropped the clothes on the floor and laid beside her. She was smiling so hard she couldn't hide it if she tried.

"Why you blushing, girl?"

"I'm not," she said grinning as she rolled her eyes and fluttered her feet.

"Lil' Tim be real. Why me? Why now? I've wanted you for all these years."

"Come on man you were a kid."

"Oh, so since I'm sixteen I can get a pass?"

"You maturing, you'll be seventeen in a few months. Now I can mold you into the perfect woman. Sexually, mentally and physically."

"But why me?"

"I genuinely love you and I know for a fact you love me. For a long time, I yearned for a woman's love because I never had it. My own mother didn't love me. I just want to experience that before it's too late. After being so close to death I realized life is too short. You're young, but I know it's real."

Kadejah leaned in and kissed me deep and passionately. "I've wanted you for so long, Tim," she whispered as I sucked on her neck.

I eased my way down to her treasure box and admired it for a few seconds my mouth began to salivate as I leaned in, inhaled her sweet scent, and attacked her love button. She squirmed, cried, yelled, and moaned then begged for the wood, but I refused. She came three times to my zero and I was cool with that, tonight was about her. Drained and satisfied she collapsed on my chest. As soon as she closed her eyes, I drifted off shortly after.

Ah'Million

Chapter 14

Donk

"What's wrong with you, nigga?" Mun asked walking through the foyer.

"I don't even want to talk about it," I spoke with my head down.

"Man tell me." He smirked.

"I lost seventy-five hundred fucking with them Cowboys last night."

"Again? You ain't going to learn until you burn. Y'all Cowboy fans die hard I never seen nothing like it," Mun continued.

"Nah, I'm done fo' real this time."

"I don't want to hear that shit cause you going to bet again next Sunday."

"As long as you know." I grinned.

"Sad, where Kadejah?"

"Arianna told me she was with Persuasia. Been with her since yesterday."

Ring! Ring! Ring!

"Who this?" I answered.

"What? Persuasia? slow down."

"Hell nah! I'm on my way."

Click!

"Aaarrrgghhh, fuck!" I screamed smashing my fist down on the wooden table.

"Donk calm the fuck down! What's wrong? Bruh, I'm here. What's wrong?"

"They got P.J. them motherfuckers killed my son man. They killed him, Mun!" I wailed.

"Who got P.J.? What happened to him? Talk to me!"

"He got shot," I whispered.

The hurt in my heart was evident the entire drive to the precinct. So many thoughts, wishes, and regrets flooded my mind. Images invaded my mental of the last time I saw him, and the words exchanged between the two of us.

I should've been the bigger person, I thought.

I bammed my fists against the steering wheel repeatedly as I continued to recant that night. I'd just made a mental note to invite P.J. over and talk to him. No man should disrespect another man's mother in their face like that. I would've done the same thing. Shit, me, I would've killed my ass if I was P.J. That was immature and selfish of me to say something like that. Not only did I disrespect him and the lady that gave him birth, but I bruised his ego and pissed on his pride.

I swerved in the lot, immediately spotting Persuasia and a young boy. I'd seen him once or twice before, but I wasn't too familiar with the kid. I parked and jumped out, killing the engine. Persuasia looked like shit, but I wasn't expecting her to look any different.

"I just had to identify his body, Donk! That was P.J. in there on that cold steel. Why? They didn't have to kill my boy!" she howled soaking my t-shirt with her tears.

I wrapped my arms around her tightly and consoled her the best way I knew how.

"Who you?" Mun asked the light-skinned kid.

"Sir, I'm Bubba, P.J.'s friend," he said with his head down.

"What the fuck happened?"

"Well, sir—"

"Before you begin, think before you speak. I'm a man of zero tolerance, me and my brother. Don't lie to me," Mun stated peering at him seriously.

"Me, P.J., and Trigga was tipped off about a house he'd been scoping out. This chick texted him and told him she had just seen everyone leave so we hurried over. P.J. discovered an unlocked window on the side of the house. He alerted us and climbed in. Trigga climbed in, and I was last to go in. As soon as I was fully inside, P.J. was in a frantic yelling at the top of his lungs that someone was inside with a gun. We all panicked and ran to the window. I climbed out as fast as I could cutting my feet on the ledge in the process. I could hear P.J. screaming hurry as I begin to yank Trigga out. I heard a gunshot and P.J.'s hand was on Trigga's back, then it fell once Trigga hopped out."

"So y'all was robbing?" I ask looking confused.

"Did you know, P?" I continued staring at her through narrow slits.

"No," she lied peering up into my eyes.

"You coming with us," I demanded

"Look you have to be strong woman. Me and Mun about to go get to the bottom of this shit. Make some motherfuckas bleed in the process. I'll get at you later, I'm sorry mama that was my son, too. But I'm about to go do something that'll make me feel better. I advise you to do the same," I voiced gripping the side of her arms while searching her eyes.

All she managed to do was nod in response and with that, I walked off.

***

"Tim! Wake up, nigga!" I spoke loudly into the phone.

"P.J. dead, me and Mun about to ride out."

"Nah, you good I understand you not all the way one-hundred percent."

"Kadejah?"

"Okay, that's even better. Keep yo' eyes on her. Meet me at the crib in an hour or two."

Tim was ready to ride and wasn't even in the position to.

"Hey, youngin!" I called out to a frightened and distraught Bubba.

"Okay, so tell me everything again," I said crossing my arms over my chest.

Bubba shook as he repeated the story, despite being a nervous wreck he included the smallest details. I was listening to everything, but blood was on my mind making it hard to concentrate.

"So, you remember how to get to that house?" I chimed in.

"No doubt."

"Let's go," Mun said buckling his seatbelt.

"It's that one right there." Bubba pointed.

I parked the car and reached for the handle.

"Chill," Mun spoke placing his hand on my chest.

"You see them, boys," he said pointing at the detectives walking from the side of the house.

"The dude with the pigs must've been the one who shot P.J. I never really got a chance to see his face," Bubba mentioned peering at the older guy talking to the detectives.

He was pointing at the window I assume that was the window P.J. climbed in.

"They better ask any and everything they can think of cause after today he won't be alive to tell shit else," Mun stated.

"Tell me the story one more time, start from when y'all awoke this morning." I attentively listened while Bubba spoke. Something about the whole thing just wasn't sitting right with me and I couldn't understand it.

"That's what I find so out of place," Mun commented

"What you talking 'bout?" I asked snapping my head into his direction.

'Your friend what's his name?"

"Trigga," Bubba answered.

"Yeah, he can lead us to whoever this bitch is so we can see why she would volunteer this falsified ass information."

"Call Trigga," I told Bubba. "Matter of fact, the element of surprise is best. Where he stay? We just gon' pull up on him," I said speeding off.

"He stays right there in Bruton Oaks with his baby mama whoever she is," Bubba said as I pulled into the apartments.

It had been a minute since I'd been in the Oaks, so long they have changed the name to some shit I can't pronounce.

"There go his truck right there, Donk," Bubba said pointing at the black Ford Escape.

"You remember which door?"

"I remember it's this section, and it's upstairs. I can't tell you if it's left or right. We'll just knock on both doors," Bubba said, unbuckling the seatbelt.

Mun and I stood behind Bubba while he knocked on the door. Someone was smoking some loud, I could smell it. Usually, it was some sort of activity going on, but it was pretty quiet today. It was still early, but that didn't mean shit.

"What up?" A boy in his early teens answered smoking a Newport with a blunt behind his ear.

His bird chest was exposed, and he wore a size too big gym shorts that hung off his waist revealing the plaid boxers. His hair resembled carpet and he still had morning boogers in the corner of his eyes.

"Trigga stay here?" Bubba asked rubbernecking past the kid.

"Nah, he across the way fam."

"Alright."

We made our way across the hall. I looked behind me to see if the kid closed the door, but just as I thought he was still watching us, being nosey. I didn't give a damn, witnesses or anyone else wasn't going to save his ass. Trigga swung the door open with a mug, but once he locked eyes with Bubba his expression softened.

"What's up, fam? Who are they?" Trigga asked looking from Mun to Donk.

"We'll talk about that in the car, come on," Mun spoke.

"Where we going? I don't know you niggas," Trigga said attempting to close the door.

Whap! In one swift motion, Mun struck Trigga in the nose with his right fist making him stumble back and crash into the table inside his crib.

"What the fuck?" The chick yelled looking our way in bewilderment.

"Look mind ya' business," I stated as Mun and I helped Trigga to his feet, out the door, and down the steps.

"Y'all niggas ain't going to get away with this!" The chick yelled from upstairs.

"Take your saggy titty ass in the house and get that shitty breath in check before you start hollering and waking folks up!" I yelled.

Shorty had a little ass on her, but she was ratchet. The weave in her head looked like the shit you could walk by and steal cause it was sold in the bins they kept on the outside of the beauty supply store.

"Get in the front, Bubba," Mun said shoving Trigga in the backseat.

Shorty was still hollering from her doorway. I wanted so badly to take aim and shoot the bitch directly between her eyes, but it was too many witnesses.

"Hey, Donk, I stay right across the street on Red Cloud."

"Who there?"

"My momma—she cool, though."

"Fuck it."

"Get out," I demanded.

We all walked up the pavement that led to Bubba's door. A few fiends were in the mix, but other than that it was dead. As soon as Bubba unlocked the door Mun shoved Trigga inside. He stumbled a little but caught his balance. Trigga looked horrified.

"Sit down," I said standing over him, while Mun took a seat and Bubba walked to the back.

"Say, I'm going to ask you a few questions and if you lie, I'm gon' pop ya head like a cork."

Trigga nodded his head in agreement.

"Who called you about the lick?"

"What lick?" he asked looking dumbfounded

Whap! Before I could react Mun backhanded him across his face instantly drawing blood.

"A girl, this little chicken head I used to fuck with. I once scoped the house out one day I was chilling with her when I saw an older guy with a suitcase and this tote. The tote resembled one like mine, that I carry my AR-15 in. So, I told the chick to call me whenever the house was clear. This morning she texted me."

"How long have you known this chick?"

"She's just a booty call, but we been fucking for about six months."

"Y'all young niggas so reckless," Mun said.

"Did y'all knock before y'all went in to assure no one was there?"

"Yes, sir, I did," Bubba spoke up.

"It's something you not telling me," Mun said peering into his eyes.

"P.J. was my nigga. I'll never put my squad in harm's way," Trigga cried.

"Watch out, Donk," Mun said standing directly in front of Trigga. "I just got one question," Mun voiced. "If we hop in that truck, right now. Would you be able to take me to the chick's house that sent you the text?"

"Hell yeah, but what does this have to do with my bitch?" Trigga hollered.

"*Your bitch?* You just said she was just a booty call. Come on let's go."

Trigga tightened his lips as the tears rolled down his face.

"What the hell going on?" Bubba's mother asked coming from the rear of the house with her scrubs on.

She looked to be in her forties, but she was beautiful a natural beauty. She was a small petite chick. She had long box braids, neatly arched eyebrows, and a nice set of teeth. She resembled Jada Pinkett in her younger days. The Set It Off and Low Down Dirty Shame days.

"Aye, ma—"

"Don't aye mama me. What y'all doing to, Trigga?" she asked looking past Bubba.

"Uh-hum," I cleared my throat. "Excuse me can I talk to you over here," I said walking off to the side.

She opened her mouth to speak, but I placed my index finger in front of my lips and motioned her towards me.

"Look P.J. got killed this morning and I believe Trigga had something to do with it. I'm not going to hurt nor kill him in your home," I assured.

"P.J.'s dead?" she asked as the crocodile tears formed in her eyes. They were so thick you would've thought they'd flood the house once they finally fell.

"Yeah, he's gone."

"Aww I'm sorry," she said wrapping her arms around my waist. I hugged her back squeezing her tiny frame.

"Hey, let's see if his word is good. We going to ride by the chicks house," Mun called out.

I slowly released Bubba's mother and walked to the door. "Bubba will be back," I assured. She nodded as I walked out behind Mun and Bubba, shutting the door behind me.

"Aye, we—"

Before I could finish my sentence, Trigga broke free from Mun's grip and jumped off the porch. He scurried down the walkway and out the gate. He moved like his life depended on it. Bubba quickly ran after him, but Trigga was too swift.

"Get that fool!" I yelled to no one in particular.

Psst! Psst! I looked over at Mun awestruck. Bubba stopped dead in his tracks once Trigga tumbled to the ground. He looked back at Mun in bewilderment.

"You said get him, that boy looked like a track star out here. I wasn't going to be able to catch him. This did, though," Mun said waving his gun while walking towards a motionless Trigga.

I looked back to see if Bubba's mother had witnessed what just occurred but luckily, she was nowhere in sight. I looked around cautiously at all the other movement but to my surprise, no one had seen it, so I thought.

"He's dead," Mun said lifting his limp and bloody body from the compound.

"Open the backseat, Bubba." Effortlessly Mun tossed Trigga in the backseat then we all climbed inside. Bubba had turned two shades lighter he was so shaken up.

"You know why he ran, right?" Mun asked using the toothpick to pick in between his teeth.

"He knew regardless he was going to die," I responded.

"No, there was either no chick or he's hiding something. He knew it was all or nothing. You didn't notice his entire disposition change when I inquired about her? No other option he took his

chance running. It's all good, cause this right here is going to con-
firm whatever suspicion we have," Mun boasted waving Trigga's
iPhone in the air.

"Okay, bet lets charge it and check it out asap."

Ring! Ring! Ring!

"Hello?" Bubba answered.

"Where you at?"

"Send me the address I'm on my way."

Click!

"Excuse me y'all, I know shit tight right now but last night
when P.J. was on his way to my crib he ran into this big producer.
Music is my everything. He convinced dude to hear me out. He
liked my flow, now he wants me to meet him at the studio."

"Give me the address," I said activating my GPS.

"You know that's the only way out, rap or play ball," Mun interjected peering out the window.

One thing I loved was the kids. Despite Bubba's lifestyle, he
was still a child. If he wanted to spread his wings I had no problem
teaching him how to fly. If this was going to pave the way so he
didn't have to rob, so be it. I wish I wouldn't have been so prideful,
but more attentive. I would've been able to peep out the shit P.J.
was doing. Bubba handed me his phone and I put the address into
my GPS. Before activating it, I called my clean-up crew to take care
of Trigga's body.

"Wadd up, boy?"

"I got this hoe in my whip and she choosing. I'm gon' hop in
your shit while you keep her company."

"Bet."

"Meet me in front of the cleaners inside Masters' shopping center."

"Give me five minutes."

Click!

Everything I discussed with my crew was in code cuz' I didn't
and never would trust this new wave of technology.

"Soon as my clean-up crew get here we gon' pull out, and one
last thing, my boy," I said turning around to face him. "If I find out

you were involved or had anything to do with P.J.'s death—your mother will be burying you beside him."

Chapter 15

Lil Tim

Kadejah and I scurried throughout the house looking for yesterday's clothes. Despite my lack of energy and strength, I moved faster than I thought.

"Lord please help P.J. in whatever trouble he has gotten himself into," Kadejah prayed aloud.

I didn't have the nuts to tell her PJ was dead so I just down-played it. Leaning against the wall I took a deep breath as I watched a distressed Kadejah. Pain was plastered all over her face. A part of me wanted to tell her the truth but I just couldn't.

"Slow down, momma. He said to meet him in an hour or two."

"It's been nearly an hour." She mugged.

"Well, with them I'm pretty sure some gangsta shit going down."

"Did you tell uncle Donk I was here?"

"Yeah, he's cool with it. Don't start tripping. Don't act scared, cause I'm going to tell them as soon as we figure things out with P.J."

"That's too soon, Lil Tim."

"It ain't no secrets between me and my dawgs. They gon' either accept it or kill me. My mind is made up. I don't want no one but you," I expressed.

"I know we did what we did, but I must tell you I'm in love with someone else."

"What?" I asked taken aback by her response. She dropped her head instead of speaking. "What nigga you done fell for?" I asked. The anger and confusion were evident as I inched a step closer.

"It's—" she hesitated.

"Spit it out," I snapped.

"It's a female! I'm in love with a bitch, Tim!" she yelled.

"Ha-ha-ha, a bitch? Kadejah you're not gay, bruh. When and how did this happen?" I spoke a bit amused.

"I know I'm not gay, but I fell for a girl in the time I spent locked up."

"You was only locked up a split second. You know what, whatever bro. Don't say I didn't try. You go ahead and shack up with ya' jail bitch. I'm gon' do my own thing," I said putting my shoes on.

"And what does that mean? What do you plan on doing?" Kadejah asked hovering over me.

"All you need to know is, I'm not doing you. Watch out," I said slightly pushing her out of my face. "Come on, let's go," I continued.

"Just like that, huh?" she asked. She stood in the middle of the living room with her hand on her hip.

"Bro you said what you said and meant it. Stand on that shit. Have the same energy when I start fucking someone else!"

"Whatever, fuck you."

"That's what you wanted me to do, but I knew you wasn't ready. That's why I didn't reward you with this good dick."

"Boy, boo," she said grabbing her purse off the table and storming out.

Kadejah and I pulled up to Donk's place, yet the driveway was still empty, so I removed my phone and sent him a text. Her confession really pissed me off, because I knew in my heart, she was the one for me. I'd never been the sentimental type. Honestly, I can't tell you what love is, because it's something I never experienced. What I do know is what I feel when I'm around Donk, Mun, and Kadejah. I know that's genuine love. The tap on Kadejah's window startled me from my thoughts. She looked quite disheveled as well.

"This your cousin?" The guy asked snatching open the door to the car.

The look on his face told me he knew Kadejah and this wasn't a stickup.

Cousin, I thought.

"Yes, this is my cousin Caleb. Did you follow me?" The guy looked over at me and slowly dropped his head in embarrassment.

"Hellooo did you follow me?" she repeated.

"What's occurring?" I sat back in my seat, head resting on my fist with my other hand inside of my jeans.

"Here, I was just bringing you this," he said tossing the phone in her lap before retreating to his car.

"Who is he?"

"Nobody."

"That don't look like a bitch to me."

Kadejah laughed at my comment and continued to look out the window. Here I was sitting here trippin' and I didn't even know what the pussy felt like.

"So, you checking me?"

"Come on man you know I been in your business before all of this other shit came about."

The sound of car doors being slammed diverted my attention, I looked back so fast I damn near broke my neck. Since being abducted I had become very paranoid and observant. I decided to keep the kidnapping a secret, because if I mentioned that I'd have to mention Caleb and I hooked up as well. Walking up the walkway I saw Donk and Kadejah lock eyes. The expression on her face must've saddened his heart cause tears fell immediately.

"Mama, I'm sorry," Donk apologized dropping his arm over her shoulders.

"Sorry? What, wha—" she asked pulling back while peering up into his eyes.

"He gone," Donk whispered.

"He's dead?" she asked looking back at me.

I wasn't even man enough to make eye contact. I eased behind Mun into the house.

"Nooo! Not my brother! Why?" She fell to her knees.

She wailed as she grabbed a hold of Donk's shirt. She cried uncontrollably with her head buried on the leg of his jeans. Donk stroked her hair to calm her grieving spirit, but it was to no avail. She hollered and slang snot for another ten minutes until she finally agreed to walk up the porch into the house where Mun and I stood in the doorway.

"Me and Mun believe P.J. was setup, but we already took care of him. We got one more to go," Mun whispered before walking further into the house.

Donk picked Kadejah up off her feet and carried her to the room.

Bing!

I looked down at the text message on my screen.

Peaches: //: Hey babe I hear you're home. I missed u! I'm at work right now. I can't call, but I'll swing by when I get off 2 get u right.

Oh, now this bitch wants to hit a nigga up.

Me: //: Nah, I'm good.

Peaches: //: Y?

Peaches: //: Don't be like that.

Peaches: //: I love you, Tim.

I slid my phone into my pocket after putting it on silent.

"Come on, Fam. We got some shit to discuss," Donk said by-passing me as he headed towards the study.

"You good?" he asked slowing his pace

"Nah, I got it." I slightly limped behind him.

Mun was already reclined on the leather sofa. I flopped down in the love seat while Donk stood in front of his desk with his hands tucked in his pockets.

"What's next?" Mun asked passing me the blunt.

"First, we take care of dude who popped P.J. Once this phone charges we can figure out how to get to the chick," Donk said pacing the floor.

"Give me a few days and I should be good to go," I assured

"Cool. Me and Mun got it covered. I'll keep you posted until then you still need Kadejah?"

"Nah, I'll be straight she took care of everything."

"You can drive?"

"Yeah, I got it."

"I'll follow you to make sure you get there safely. When I come back bro, we can go handle that."

118

"Bet."

Ah'Million

Chapter 16

Bubba

I was still shaking once I was inside the studio after Mun and Donk dropped me off. I don't recall a time I'd been that afraid. P.J. always spoke highly about both men especially Donk, but I had never met them or witnessed it for myself. My heart saddened as I thought about it all. My feet still ached from climbing out the window in a hurry. Once I hopped off the ledge, I begin to yank Trigga out when I heard the thunderous noise. I knew it had to be a shotgun.

Then I saw P.J.'s hand grip Trigga's t-shirt. He hung on for dear life as Trigga struggled out of the window, but I heard the noise again and P.J.'s hand went limp vanishing from my sight. Trigga leaped off the ledge in time and took off. I stood there, stuck. The inside of the house was so dark I couldn't even see, but I just knew my boy was gone.

It should've been me instead of P.J. I was the greedy one. I was the one that wanted to go even after he told me he was good. P.J. was just in love with the adrenaline rush and the beauty of it because money wasn't an issue. He used to tell me how he wanted to man up and take care of his mother and sister but Persuasia hopped on enough poles to take care of herself. Donk would give P.J. anything he asked for, but as he aged, he grew tired of asking.

At young ages, mothers instill in young boys that they were the men of the house if pops isn't around. It stuck with me just like it stuck with him. What man wants to approach another man for a handout. Although neither of us are grown, but what momma say goes.

Rah led me to the sofa. "Listen to this beat, let it simmer. I'm going to play it twice more after this. I want you to hop on the beat. Fresh off the dome. If not feeling it, I got pen and paper over there."

"Bet," I said without looking up. I was trying to focus on the beat, but my mind drifted off to Trigga.

Would he really do something so grimy? I thought.

Ah'Million

I needed something to prove it. I'd known Trigga a long time and never questioned his loyalty. A tear fell from my eye and I quickly swiped it away. If I didn't know nothing else, I knew I was going to miss my dawgs. I could hear Rah restart the track.

"Hey, you can stop it," I said standing to my feet.

"You sure? I only played it once. You got two more times," Rah explained.

"Nah, I'm ready."

"You ready? Okay, drop the beat."

I bobbed as the music played. I took a swig of the Dasani and let it rip.

"Daddy gave it to me raw,
He ain't give me a dime
That shit hurt my soul
So I'ma' say it one mo' time
Cuz if it wasn't for my T lady
I wouldn't have even made it
Cops, they tryin' to take me
Hoes, want to plant a baby
Same hoes from before that didn't know a nigga
I don't beef on social media I'll front doe' you nigga
Skinny jeans with the ashy knees I couldn't afford Hilfiger
To, later on, find out the dude Tommy don't like niggas
So, it's Polo til' I go ho'
Paid now ain't' going broke no mo'
Took my nigga life over a flat yo'
Death is something you can't get back bro. Shit cray cray
One wish like Ray J and my dawg would be here today
We headed down that street with that piece just tryin' to eat
Shots rang out like a beat, left my dawg sprawled on the concrete
You show love, they'll give hate
They turn fo' cause they been fake
As long as I got it yo' sista straight
I love you, RIP P.J."

"Stop! I said stop got damnit. Wheeew!" Rah yelled fanning me with his napkin.

"He the truth, Rah!" the few dudes sitting around the studio yelled

"Aye, step outside with me." I followed Rah outside the noisy studio. "Hey, man you wrote that?" Rah asked rocking on the tip of his toes.

"Nah. It's mine but I didn't write it. You wanted something right off the dome so that's what I gave you."

"It was filled with so much emotion, that shit was lit. I noticed you had tears in your eyes, youngblood. You good?"

"Yeah, my fam got killed yesterday. The one you met at the store that introduced us to one another."

"Word?" he asked shaking his head.

"Yeah."

"Y'all have money for the funeral?"

"Yeah, we good on that."

"Look I been thinking, I done talked to a few people. How would you like to be your own man making more money than you can count?"

"Hell yeah! Where do I sign?"

"On the dotted line, come on." I followed Rah back inside and into his office.

I could still hear the dudes outside the office discussing my bars. I took the thin stack of papers scanned through the pages and immediately signed on the dotted line.

"I have a few artists lined up and I'll get them on the line today to see what's up."

"Hell yeah, it's already artists that want to do a collab?"

"Nah, its artist that need bars."

"Bars?"

"Lyrics, writers," Rah responded dryly.

"What that got to do with me?"

"You're a ghostwriter."

"A ghostwriter? I don't want to be a damn ghostwriter.

"You are now."

"What you mean, I am now? Hold the fuck up!" I yelled standing to my feet.

"Nah, you calm the fuck down. You signed on the dotted line. It's no longer up to you."

"Fo' real dawg, you just gon' play me like that?"

"I didn't play you, you played yourself you should've read the contract."

"Fuck you and that contract. You can eat the shit out of my ass," I stated slamming the door shut behind me and barging out of the studio.

I knew I was gifted with this shit and if I wasn't determined before I definitely was now. This shit bigger than me and I know P.J. still wanted a nigga to make it with this rap shit. That's why I'm gon' blow if it's the last thing I do. This one for you, baby.

Chapter 17

Bando

I was so glad to see my dawg home, only thing, he wasn't 100%, it sort of fucked with me until he assured me he'd be well real soon. Lil Tim and I were more than boys we were like brothers. Since day one the trust was there. One night I made a move to the Exxon across the way, that I had been scoping for the past few weeks when I spotted Lil Tim exit the store. He was ambushed by more than a few men, reluctantly I hopped out, letting my uzi spit. A few were hit, one died, and the rest scattered like roaches. We been thugging since then.

'Hey, Bando! Your baby mother outside!" Ms. Jan's nosey ass yelled.

Ms. Jan didn't miss a beat. She saw and heard everything. I was becoming sick of Liz's washed up ass. Since I hit her spot, she'd been blowing up my spot. She was merely a typical one-night-stand. The night I met her, she was tipsy, but she knew how to handle the liquor. She was rambunctious and ghetto, and now since I'd been ducking her ass, she hates me with a passion.

"You need to stop playing games with me," she spoke in broken English as she waddled closer, the seed inside her forced her to walk like a penguin. Six months pregnant and it did nothing but enhance her beauty.

Beauty isn't rare like it used to be. So many tools you can use for enhancements. If you're ugly and your ass flat, you in last place. Cosmetic surgeons are in competition. You have Dr. Atlanta charging a thousand less than Dr. Miami and Dr. Austin doing buy an ass get breast free specials. Honestly, I don't give a damn about any of that. I do love a woman easy on the eyes, but the majority of those women hurt you. Give me trust, loyalty, and affection. I don't need the baddest. Get jammed up and see which of the two go astray.

"What you want, Liz?"

"So, you not going to try and be part of your son's life at all?"

Son? Bitches kill me. Now all of a sudden, she claiming the gender. This bitch hasn't seen no doctor. She just making shit up. Knowing a boy is every man's dream.

"Is this what you wanted?"

"No, I wanted to know if you're going to be at the hospital the day I deliver your seed?"

"Naw. Why would I do that? That's not my job."

"The father is allowed inside."

"Exactly, I'm not the father! That's not my seed!"

"Tuh, you deadbeats," she voiced shaking her head

"Nah, you trash bags. Fuck every nigga in the hood then plant the baby on the guy with the most loot," I continued. Liz quickly swung barely missing my face. "What the fuck?" I asked looking at her shocked.

"I hate you!" she wailed.

The neighbors across the street were standing on their porch being nosey. I couldn't be mad at them if it was someone else, I'd be doing the same shit.

"Liz, chill with that bull shit. I'm about to leave you standing out here!" I yelled grabbing her arms aggressively.

Her mascara, eyeliner, and whatever the fuck it was descended down her face landing directly on top of her red lipstick. For a second, she scared me as she continued to curse at the top of her lungs resembling the clown Pennywise.

"Bruh, what the fuck you want from me?" I asked gripping my head in frustration.

Her cries and sniffles ceased abruptly as she used the back of her hand to wipe the snot from her nose.

"I have a proposition for you," she said.

***

"What's up, boy!" Lil Tim greeted me at the door.

"What's good, baby," I responded as we quickly embraced before stepping inside his apartment.

"Damn, nigga why you got it so dark in here?"

"I was laying down. Where you coming from?"

"Well, I had met this chick named, Liz at the club one night. I hit her and forgot about her. Four months later she comes out of hiding and tells me I'm the baby's daddy. I been keeping her at bay so I can nip the shit in the bud once the baby is born and we take a DNA test. So, then she tells me she will abort the baby if I give her six racks. I been waiting to hear that for the longest. I did hit the bitch raw, Fam," I admitted with a boyish grin.

"Liz? Liz," Lil Tim repeated trying to search his memory bank. "I don't know her but stay strapped. These females aren't to be trusted. I'm living proof." He chuckled.

"You feeling better?"

"A little every day I improve. I should be at one-hundred-percent in two days."

"I brought you some Long John Silvers."

"Hell yeah, I was just about to order something." I handed Tim the bag of food. "It's pretty clean for you to barely be able to walk."

"Kadejah did that yesterday."

"Oh, okay, I really haven't seen her little ass since she came home from Juvy."

"Her badass been ducked off," Tim responded, he looked to be in deep thought.

"So, now that you're home. What's your next move?"

"Once I get right it's back to the basics, doing what I do best. Mun's here now, I don't know what part he plays, but I'm not pressed. It's enough money for us all."

"You damn right, I can't wait for you to shake back. I miss you boy. You know the prairie view game in two weeks, hopefully, we can slide through and bag some bitches like we always do."

"Hell yeah, I haven't turnt up since the night I went missing. Shit, I probably need to leave these hoes alone?"

"Did you find out who it was?"

"Yeah, Meech's little sister."

"Mariyah?"

"Yeah, you know her?" he asked scanning my eyes.

"Nah, you told me about her," I quickly responded.

"That's right."

"Well, fam, I love you. I'll holler at you later. I have to head to the spot."

"The new cat straight?"

"Twan? Yeah, he persistent. Sort of remind you of Reggie."

"Nah, it'll never be another Reggie."

"You sure, right."

Chapter 18

Mun

Ding! Ding! Ding!

Donk and I hid behind the wooden chair to avoid being seen, just in case someone was looking out of the peephole.

"Ring it again," Donk whispered.

I stood up and crept to the doorbell, ringing it twice. I could hear the locks turning from inside the house. Guns in hand we waited for the door to open, but there was a long pause. No doors opening, no sound whatsoever. I found it kind of awkward, however, Donk and I remained in position. The faint sound of the door opening caught my attention and before I could nudge Donk he flew to his feet and I followed suit.

"What's going on?" the dude hollered evidently shocked.

We rushed him inside with our pistols drawn. The same shotty he used on P.J. earlier was in his hands. Donk pistol-whipped him to cease his concerns, he instantly lost grip of the shotty and it fell to the floor.

"Sit your ass down," Donk demanded while I scurried through the house looking for a light switch.

I switch on the lights immediately spotting the dead wild animal heads that decorated the walls.

"What do you want, sir? I hunt for a living. I have no money, just a lot of meat!"

"I don't want no squirrel, deer, or whatever else you're offering. Why the fuck you kill my son?"

The jerking and squirming even the sniffles ceased as soon as the words fell from my lips. He dropped his head in defeat.

Whap!

Blood trickled down his temple as soon as I connected the metal with it.

"Answer him or the next one's going to blind your old ass," I threatened. I really just wanted to pop his fat ass and be done with it.

"I was paid to hide out and wait for some guys to rob my house. I was ordered to shoot the first one who came in through the window on the right." My eyes narrowed as I peered at Donk. I knew this shit was deeper than it looked.

"Who paid you?"

"A young chick. We never discussed her name or any personal information, just money."

"You lying to me?" Donk asked, grabbing the collar of his shirt.

"No, sir."

"How did you contact her?" Donk ask while I patted his pockets for his phone.

"It's the last number on my call log."

I called the number and placed it on speaker.

"Tell her to meet you somewhere you have important information for her," I mouthed peering into his eyes.

He quickly nodded his head assuring his willingness to cooperate but it was too late for that. He was good as dead.

"Hello?"

"The detectives just left. I need to speak with you immediately. Could you meet me somewhere?"

"You're home?" she asked

"Yes."

"Meet me at the Minyards on Masters."

"Okay, bye."

Boom! Boom! Boom!

I placed the barrel of the 9mm underneath his eye and fired three shots into his face sending pieces of his flesh flying.

"Now when the laws come to investigate you won't have shit to say."

The lot was spacious and quite crowded. I texted the chick the whole ride there to avoid talking over the phone and her picking up on my voice.

//: I'm here. she texted.

"She's here did you just see someone pull in?" I ask Donk.

"No female, just that little dude over there, but he's riding alone you can see inside his car."

Me: //: I don't c u.

Ring! Ring!

"Shit, she's calling bro."

"Well, you sound nothing like the dude. So, you can't answer it."

I let the phone ring until it stopped.

Her: //: Why you not picking up?

"Where is she I don't see her," Donk said scanning the lot.

Her: //: U trying 2 set me up?

"Fuck, she on to us," I voiced.

"Well, I don't see no one, I'm leaving."

Her: //: I'm gone.

"She's leaving!" I peered around frantically, it was four cars veering out into the intersection. "Fuck!" I said

"It's cool Trigga's phone will help us find her."

***

"Girl get in this car," I joked while waiting.

Bry did a full three-sixty outside of the car peering through the driver's side window.

"Don't act like you not enjoying the view. I have to make sure I'm good before we go to this movie theatre," she explained climbing into the passenger seat.

Bry was gorgeous, her skin tone was a golden, creamy complexion. Her lips were pink and succulent. Although, Bry was a natural beauty she loved makeup.

"What's on your mind?" Bry asked peering at me with her beautiful, chestnut brown eyes. Her green and copper eyeshadow matched them.

"I'm cool. Why you ask that?"

"You seem a little off tonight"

Bry and I had been conversing for nearly two weeks now, yet, I still didn't feel comfortable exposing any of my personal business.

Bry's grimy antics and disloyalty was part of the reason I had trust issues. The love I had for her allowed me to have mercy and compassion, compelling me to drop my guard, cause I did something I'd never done before which was give a bitch a second chance. I should've cut her off when she came clean about her inability to have kids, after faking pregnancies and miscarriages the entire time. Fucking with that crazy bitch almost cost me my life.

"I told you, I'm straight ma. Let's go," I said unbuckling my seat belt.

Bry climbed out of the whip after tucking her sheepskin Chanel bag underneath the seat.

"Oh, you just leave your bag and shit? You have no plans on spending any money, huh?" I joked.

The white fitted Gucci shirt and cargo joggers complimented her slim thick figure. She tossed her bundles to the back and strutted across the lot. She had a runway walk with legs like Ciara.

"Bae you never decided, *Us* or *Hustlers*? she asked.

"Whatever you want to watch beautiful."

"Can we have tickets to see *Us* please?"

I really didn't care which of the two but let me find out she didn't want me to see Cardi and J-Lo raw and uncut. Bry and I headed inside with a large group of people, I'm surprised I didn't see any familiar faces. After retrieving drinks and snacks we made our way to our seats. We laughed and engaged in deep conversations during the movie trailers.

"Ooohhh, bae, it's on," she said tapping me on my arm.

I tried looking away, but my eyes were glued. The guy across the way looked all too familiar and I couldn't hide the dread written all over my face.

"Mun!" Bry yelled, finally snapping me out of my trance.

"Huh?"

"Who are you looking at?" she asked trying to follow my eyes. She rammed back in her seat, crossing her arms at her chest. It was evident she was upset.

"Come on, that childish shit don't look good on you, ma," I voiced draping my arm over her shoulder.

Like a kid engrossed in a cartoon. Bry never took her eyes off the screen. I would seldomly cut my eyes in his direction. Although his physical appearance had totally changed, I'd never forget those sneaky, black, beady eyes. Being that the theatre was so dark that's all I could see anyways. I pulled my phone out on the sly, I figured if I texted Donk I could have him on the outside just in case dude tried something after the movie, but before I could finish the text an incoming call came in.

He must have been feeling the uneasiness, I thought, staring down at Donk's name on my screen.

"Yo?"

"Fam, where you at?" he asked with urgency

"I'm at the movies with my shorty. Why what's up?"

"Did you know about Kadejah lil' ass having a fake I.D? The hell she trying to do?"

"She thinks she's grown. We'll figure it out. Look I was just about to text you and tell you to meet me up here."

"Up where?"

"AMC Thirty."

"Why what's up?"

"Juanito caught me slipping, he about four rows to the left of me and I'm sure he might try so—"

Bock! Bock! Bock!

"Aagghhh!"

The piercing sound rang out throughout the theatre everyone took off in different directions, screaming and shoving each other. I grabbed Bry by the hand and headed toward the exit. Shots whizzed past my head. I immediately thought of Bry and became upset with myself for putting her in a situation like this knowing I was a wanted man.

"Aaagghhh!"

"Get down and low, Bry!"

Boom! Boom! Boom!

"Bae, get low!" I hollered using my body to shield her while we walked, crouched down toward the exit.

"Fuck!" The guy next to me yelped out as a bullet struck him in the ear.

Blood splattered down on me from above as Bry led the way through the crowd. We pushed our way through and into the hallway. I noticed some bulky dudes standing at the entryway staring into my direction, so I veered into the opposite direction of the exit dragging Bry along.

I'd rather take my chances riding out and hope the police will arrive, I thought.

"Stand up and run bae, come on," I said as we took off running down the hall

The Lion King PG-13 The sign read. I pulled the doors open and just as I expected it was empty.

"Come on!" We flew down the steps all the way to the first row in front of the screen.

"You go in between the row and lay down." Shaken up but still quick on her toes, Bry did exactly what I instructed, while I laid down directly on top of her.

"Mun," she whispered while sniffling.

"Yeah?"

"Are those guys after you?"

"Yeah, mama, I'll tell you about it later."

The voices outside the door were faint due to the volume of the movie but I could still hear screaming.

"Come on! Y'all two go and check the movie across the hallway." I knew that voice, it belonged to Joey one of Juanito's foot soldiers. He must've moved up in rank since the disappearance of his two best men.

"Check every area and every row of seats! This motherfucker is still here somewhere!"

I could hear them making their way around the room by the sound of things. They weren't close but soon enough they would be, sweat beads dripped down my forehead. I had to think of something, and fast. The .22 in my sock was no match for these guys, but I didn't want to risk bringing anything bigger in the theatre. I could hear footsteps approaching.

134

"Look, I'm going to get up and shoot to distract them. You slide out and stay low until you find your way out."

She nodded her head as the tears cascaded down her face knowing I put her in harm's way. I'd rather die trying to help her out.

"You got this, ma—"

Boom! Boom! Boom!

Tit! Tit! Tit! Tit! Tit! Tit! Tit!

"Aaarrgghh." I looked into the empty eyes of Joey as he collapsed on his side with smoke rising from his body. He fell directly in front of the row we hid in between. I stared into his lifeless eyes afraid to move.

"Where my motherfucking brother at?" Donk yelled, his voice full of anger, sadness, and frustration.

I peeked up from in between the seats like a badass kid who had been doing something he didn't have any business.

"Donk!" I yelled grinning as I stood to my feet, pulling Bry up to hers. I quickly removed Joey's pistol from his waist and jogged towards Donk.

"Aye, it's quite a few of them. I'm so happy to see you. Yo' black ass always on time."

"I killed four of them already. Well, five now, because there were three guarding the entrance."

"It's more with Juanito."

"Okay, come on."

The three of us crept out of the room and into the hallway. No one was in sight. We quickened our pace down the hall and paused when he heard voices coming from around the corner. Donk put up his finger as he inched closer to the edge. He leaned up against the wall and peeked around the corner.

"It's Juanito and his men. They're running for the exit. I hear sirens!"

"You don't want to get at his old ass while we can?" Mun suggested.

"Nah, we have to find another exit asap! I can't go back, Fam!"

"Follow me," Bry said jogging past us.

Donk and I looked at one another before running behind her.

"How you know where you going, girl?"

"I used to work here."

The three of us bent the corner and hurried down the short hallway. To the left was a door that read: *Emergency Exit*. Bry twisted the knob but it didn't open.

"Move," Donk said while aiming at the knob.

Boom!

The door swung open and we took off towards the massive crowd. I peered around for Juanito as we blended in with everyone else. Police cars were everywhere a few of them rushed inside.

"Let's get out of here, I parked over there," Donk said leading the way.

***

When we got to my house and went inside and sat down, I peered over at Bry. Her face was swollen and puffy. Her small button nose was ruby red.

"You alright, mama?" I ask rubbing her thigh.

"Yeah, bae, I'm good. I just didn't think the night would end like this."

"I know, it was truly unexpected, I'm sorry. Can I try again tomorrow?"

"Tomorrow?" she repeated with a wide eye expression.

I dropped my head in embarrassment, I couldn't blame her.

"I'll go, but you have to promise to protect me like you did today."

"You must be really feeling a nigga. Cuz' you said that without hesitation and you almost lost your life ten minutes ago."

She chuckled using the back of her hand to wipe her eyes.

"Come on, you ready?"

"Yes," I replied.

"Donk?"

"Yeah!"

"I'll be back!"

"Bet."

Chapter 19

Arianna

I received the devastating news about P.J. the other day. My spirit was beyond crushed. I instantly felt guilty for leaving him alone in my room that night. I should've stayed with him like he wanted me to, but I was so into Quincy that I put P.J. on the back burner. Even though P.J. was there when I needed him most and that's why I fell for him the way I did. He just never really felt the same about me, if so, he had a weird way of showing it. Everyone was so distracted with P.J.'s death, Donk didn't notice the two nights I snuck out.

Me and Quincy would chill, watch movies, have baby-making sex, and the next day he would swing by the job and chill with me for a little while. Quincy was controlling, but I liked him, and he liked me. He just wanted what was best for me. I pondered on the idea of telling Uncle Donk about him but I decided against it. Quincy was nearly triple my age and Uncle Donk would probably kill him for even thinking we could be together. Honestly, I believe I'm in love. Kadejah thinks it's lust. He even bought me expensive gifts like diamond earrings and a tennis bracelet. He spoiled me with attention and affection.

"I need some fresh air. You want to go to cheddars tonight?" Despite the tough act, I could see the misery in Kadejah's eyes. Today was the first day she'd shown her face outside her room since P.J.'s death.

"Yeah, let me ask Quincy," I responded.

"*Ask Quincy*? Y'all are one?"

"Yes, girl."

"Oh, I have to meet him. I assume he's the one who put the diamonds in your ear and around your wrist?"

"He sure did," I replied while shooting a message to Quincy.

Me: //: Can I go 2 cheddars 2night with my sis?

I slid the phone into my pocket and wiped off the counter.

"Here go this bitch," Kadejah mumbled as the lady walked in.

Every day around the same time she would stop by. Kadejah thinks she has a motive. I believe she's just lonely.

"I got this. How may I help you?"

"Yes, can I have two Banana Nut muffins and a large Frappe with extra caramel syrup on top?"

"Oh, new order today?" Kadejah asked.

Instead of responding she peered at Kadejah with a deadpan expression, startling the hell out of me.

Bzz! Bzz! Bzz!

Quincy: //: No, I have plans 4 us 2 night.

Me: //: Can I invite my sis?

"Dan, let me have two Banana Nut muffins!" I yelled while making the Frappe.

Bzz! Bzz! Bzz!

Quincy: //: I said No! I'll call you at 7.

I dropped the phone in my pocket and passed the Frappe to Kadejah. She took the lady her order and said something quick before walking away.

"Look, I can't go tonight. Maybe we can plan something for tomorrow?"

"Oh, daddy said, no? He got you on lock? It's cool, I'll do my own thing." If P.J. was alive Kadejah wouldn't have asked me to go. She really don't ask me for much anyways. The least I could do was support her at a time like this.

"Sis, he don't own me we can go to cheddars and anywhere else you want to go."

"Now, that's the Arianna I know."

"Amy don't get boogie, bitch. The only reason you're here is cuz' we needed a set of wheels," Kadejah voiced loudly while waiting to be seated.

It was packed inside the restaurant like a can of sardines. The five-inch pumps were hurting my feet and we hadn't been inside ten minutes.

"I know you don't fool with me like that. There's no need to remind me, Kadejah," Amy spoke sadly.

"Girl, boo."

"Ladies right this way," the scrawny male waiter announced as he led us through the busy restaurant.

We bypassed Newlyweds, old couples, a group of people celebrating a birthday, and teens who had all their belongings in their hands looking for the best time to run out. The waiter kept looking back at the table full of teens.

"Are you ladies ready to place your order?"

While placing the order, I watched the teens tiptoe out of the restaurant. All I could do was shake my head.

"Okay, I'll be back with your food shortly," he said walking off.

"Fuck not again!" he yelled while swiftly scanning the table for cash, but nothing was there only dirty dishes. Some emptier than others.

"They still do that?" Amy asked looking back.

"That shit is so whack, right, Kadejah?" Kadejah looked completely zoned out. "What's wrong, sis?"

"I miss P.J. and Tru," she whined.

I wasn't great at consoling, so I gently rubbed her back. I almost choked on my glass of water when I spotted Quincy walking towards my table. My eyes grew double their normal size and I instantly begin to panic. Kadejah must've picked up on my uneasiness but before she could speak Quincy was standing in front of our table with his hands in his pockets.

How did he know I was here? I thought

"Hey, beautiful. How are y'all ladies? I'm Quincy."

"Oh, heeyyy, Quincy!" Kadejah yelled in excitement while Amy continued to nurse her water.

"Hello, Ms. Kadejah, it is a pleasure meeting you. I've heard nothing but wonderful things about you, baby girl. Baby, can I speak with you outside real quick?"

"Of course, baby," I agreed sitting my clutch on the table.

Kadejah was smiling like a proud parent on prom night. Amy was in her feelings if you ask me. Quincy grabbed me by the hand, and we walked outside into the cold night.

"Let's sit in the car so I can taste those sweet lips." I hurried to the car to show my man some love and affection.

Whack!

As soon as the car door slammed Quincy backhanded me connecting with my ear. For a minute I thought I'd lost my hearing. I looked over at Quincy who was ranting and raving, but I couldn't hear anything he was saying only the ringing in my ear. I placed my hand over my ear in disbelief it was so warm I thought I would burn my hand. I rubbed around my ear for swelling. Tears welled up in my eyes and I instantly regretted getting involved with Quincy.

"Why did you hit me, Quincy? What did I do? Why are you so upset? That's my sister in there."

"I don't give a damn if it was your mama. I told you, I had plans for us. You ignore what I say and bring yo' ass up here anyways."

"I didn't think you would have a problem with it being it's just my sister. She needs me, Quincy. You know our brother just passed." Quincy lowered his head.

"You right, I'm sorry, baby girl. Let me make it up to you," he offered.

"We can talk about it tomorrow," I said reaching for the door handle.

"No, I want to take you back to my place. Let's talk about it now."

"Quincy, I have to go back ins—" He pressed the button to lock the doors and started the engine.

"Quincy, my purse in there!"

"It's okay your sister will get it. Shoot her text and tell her you left with me."

I done fell for a fucking psychopath, I thought while peering out of the window.

I removed my phone from my bra and text Kadejah as I enjoyed the breeze coming through the small crack in the window.

I removed my pumps and sat on the sofa. Quincy was right on my heels. I was still upset about everything that had occurred. My ear still ached, and I was now feeling the *low*. Persuasia taught me a thing or two about love. She said it's a high that'll have you thinking you're walking on clouds, but then there's a low, so low it'll retain all your energy, time, focus, strength, joy and peace, drain you of everything you've worked for. At this moment I felt exactly like that. Quincy dropped the keys on the table and tilted my head upwards with his finger. I felt so disgusted.

"I'll be back." I removed my strapless dress and pinned my curly hair up.

"Come here," Quincy demanded with a towel filled with ice.

I straddled his lap laying my head on his shoulder as he sat the cold towel on my ear. From time to time he would plant soft pecks on my forehead, but he never removed the towel. My eyelids grew heavy and before long I was out cold. I awoke to my clitoris thumping. Quincy was massaging it through my panties. I let out a soft moan and he whipped out his rock-hard penis. He swiftly yanked my panties to the side and entered me slowly. His thrusts were deep and sweet. Like dope to a fiend, food to homeless man, designer to a bad bitch, I needed this. A feeling so magnificent and pleasurable. A single tear fell from my eye and I knew I was in it for the long haul. I immediately forgot about the verbal and physical abuse and I was back feeling that *high*. Low? What low? What's that?

"You mine," he whispered wrapping his hand around my throat as he plunged my insides slow and deeply.

"Yes, I'm all yours Quincy. I'm sorry for, for what I did."

"You not gon' do it again, huh?"

"No more, I promise."

"You what?" He thrust harder

"I promise!" I yelped out

"You gon' move in?"

"Yes, daddy whatever you want."

Ah'Million

Chapter 20

Bando

The cash hadn't been flowing in the way I wanted it to, but it was still flowing. Slow cash beats *no* cash any day. My OG used to tell me *faster the cash, quicker the crash*. I still did things my way. The spot was booming like the welfare office, but with my expensive habits, progression was slow. The Crown Royal XR was simply smooth.

"Donk if you cool with it, I'm going to head out. I just got a call and I hear the traffic is pretty thick down the way. So, I'm going to open up shop," Twan said. If Twan didn't have anything else, he had ambition.

"Cool. You don't want to eat first?"

"Nah, I'm good, I'll have something to go."

"Alright, Money, be careful. Niggas starving and they'll eat off anyone plate whether you're offering it or they're taking it." Donk was right times had changed and the streets weren't as safe as they used to be.

Lately, I'd been packing not one but two pistols. I remember days you could chill outside all times of the night, play games like hide go get it and tag. Momma yelling your name because you sup-posed to beat the street lights which was hard cause the night time was the best time to play.

One night my mother caught me goosing a chick red-handed. I was pumping her from the back, covered in sweat, and nearly out of breath. Yet, I was fully clothed. I heard the footsteps in the grass, but the way shorty was moaning and backing it up I thought it was her.

"Brandon!" she yelled and before I could turn around good, I felt a strong palm connect with the back of my bald head.

My mother shaved my head because my cousin who was a few years older than me told me he could cut. I let him and he patched me up. It was a mess, so bad my shit resembled a globe. Instead of a multitude of colors, there was a multitude of bald spots. So, my mother shaved it bald. A week straight I was teased non-stop. I almost got into a fight with Lil' Eddie, a younger kid who stayed in the other section of the apartments.

"Get yo' milk dud head ass, shitty, brown acorn head ass," dude went on and on and on.

I wanted to fight him, but he was four years younger than me. The baby of the bunch and I wouldn't have got any cool points for beating up lil' Eddie. After my mother nearly cocked my eyes with that hit, she grabbed me by the ear and led me inside. Shorty took off running before my mother could identify her. Once I was inside, I had to stand in the corner as a form of punishment. She would walk in and out of the living room, so every time she'd walk in, I'd place my hand behind my back and even my posture. Hoping she'd have sympathy being that I'm doing it correctly, but I was wrong.

"Bando?"

"Bando?"

"Huh? My bad I was thinking about something."

"Shit, I see, it's time for you to order," Donk said.

"Bet, let me see," I replied rubbing my palms together.

"Man, shorty looking right."

Damn, who is that? I thought as I watched Mun's date sit down at the table.

Tonight, Donk invited the squad to Pappadeaux everything on him. Donk and I showed up alone. Mun walked in with a bad bitch and Lil' Tim brought Peaches ho' ass. I really didn't want my boy fucking with her dawg ass being that she was recently with Melo's cutthroat ass. Piss a bitch off and they'll turn on you like they never knew you.

Once everyone arrived and greeted each other, Donk stood to his feet. Dressed in a cream-colored Tom Ford jacket, gray Tom Ford sweater, and pants with a pair of Christian Louboutin loafers. I removed the Olive-green, Christian Dior scarf and sat attentively at the long table.

"I um—" he began placing his hands in his pockets.

"You know recently I lost someone real close to me and I just want to show a little love, cause I haven't shown my appreciation lately. Life is too short for the bullshit. Excluding the women here y'all are my soldiers. I love y'all. Y'all my niggas til' the tagz," he announced before taking his seat.

"We love you, too," the rest of us shouted in unison while giving him a round of applause.

"What would you all like to drink? I'll be back to take your food order," the waitress spoke. She was a bit on the chubby side, but she had a pretty face.

"Bring us a bottle of that Louis XIII Cognac and a bottle of that Ace of Spade. Would you ladies like something fruity?"

"Oh, I'm cool. I don't hardly drink," Bry responded.

"Nah, I can hang," Peaches said.

I peered over at her greedy ass. I don't know what Tim was thinking of bringing her here. Only wifey's meet the Fam.

"So, fam did Donk tell you your new position?" I spoke in a low tone to Lil' Tim who sat directly beside me.

Although he was with Peaches, he paid her no attention. She kept giving me the side-eye, but I ignored her ho' ass.

"He's working on something new out there in the boondocks. Strictly pills and weed. He wants me to be head of the operation, just looking for a few workers."

"That's what's—"

"Bando," Donk chimed in.

I peered up at him as he signaled me over.

"What's up, Fam?" I asked once I was in earshot.

He stood to his feet while scanning the crowd.

"You good?" he asked

"Yeah, I'm straight. Just a little fucked up 'bout P.J.,"

He probably thought I was changing on him. That wasn't the case I just had to ride solo to keep him out of harm's way"

"I understand. It's really a sensitive topic. I called you up here to see if you had plans of retiring?"

"Hell nah, fam I'm doing this shit til' I get gray."

"That's why I chose you for the job. I don't need anyone in this line of field that's skeptical." I tried to hide my excitement when he mentioned the word job.

"Mun and I are about to make some legit moves. Tim is going to take Mun spot and I want you in charge of the new spot out in the boondocks."

"Okay, I got you."

"You got a lot of heart and you're determined," he spoke at a low tone.

"Big homie, I really appreciate this."

"No problem, I'll give you the rundown on everything sometime next week. Until then keep doing what you doing."

"Bet."

"Hey, is Twan legit?" He pried scanning my eyes.

Donk's eyes pierced your soul. Making you nervous. I played it off lifting my feet peering down at my shoe as if I stepped in something.

"I like Twan. He's direct and focused. Always down for the cause and he's not on no slick shit. I have a test of my own."

"Okay, cool, I'm tired of getting money with the op. I've done enough of that already. You say he good then that's what it is. Let's celebrate!"

Chapter 21

Kadejah

I sat in front of the church, black Dior shades covered my eyes. There was no sign of Tim or Arianna. Persuasia, Donk, Mun, Bubba, Bando, and I were in attendance. The pastor was saying whatever pastors say at funerals but the words fell on deaf ears. I stared at the closed casket engrossed in thought. It's a shame I couldn't see his handsome face.

Persuasia must've been outselling ass all night because she was the last to arrive. I assumed our once broken family would all become one since P.J.'s death, but Uncle Donk seemed to hate Persuasia now more than ever. He wouldn't even console or hold her. I draped my arm over her shoulder to show compassion, but it only made it worse as her cries grew into a loud sustained doleful sound.

Arianna on the other hand, I haven't seen or heard from her since she ran out of Cheddar's with that overgrown ass dude. He had to be at least in his mid-thirties. Don't get me wrong he was handsome, but he wasn't fooling me. The church doors swung open and immediately everyone turned around. I did a double-take when I spotted Peaches and Lil' Tim, shocked I removed my shades.

"I know he didn't just walk his ass up in here with this bitch like she's apart of the fam," I mumbled.

"What you say, baby?" Uncle Donk asked leaning over towards me.

"Oh, nothing Unc. I was praying," I lied.

Lil' Tim walked smoothly up the aisle. I was fuming on the inside and wanted to spaz out on both of them. He nodded and Peaches flashed a smile before taking their seats next to Mun.

"What up, boy?" They replied.

I didn't acknowledge him or his chick. Donk nudged me in the arm with his elbow but I ignored him too. I was tired of doing shit I didn't feel like doing. Faking the funk, fuck that. The pianist began to play the familiar tune and I just knew my ears were deceiving me until the song kicked in from the speakers. *Wiz Khalifa's See You*

Again blasted throughout the church as the tears welled up in my eyes.

The projector came to life and the slide show started. I figured Persuasia put this part together personally because there were images of P.J. and I that I didn't recall taking, images of the four of us as a family. I looked to the right at Uncle Donk who had tears gliding down his smooth dark skin.

"No, no, no, no. Oh, God!" I pleaded with my face buried in the palm of my hands using my tongue to remove the snot that had fallen onto my lip.

I couldn't control my sniffles. I wasn't prepared for this at all. Just when I thought I was strong I peeked up at P.J. and I on our first day of school, the year he begged Persuasia to let him attend my school. Oddly, he ended up doing so, but as I watched us peer down the long hallway at Donk and Persuasia headed into a separate direction. I leaped from my seat and ran out of the church. I couldn't stomach the shit for another second. I wanted to curse God cause he had the power to prevent it. I wanted to curse P.J. for leaving me. I wanted to curse Arianna for being absent. However, it wasn't anyone's fault that we live in a world of tragedy. A world of wickedness, illness, death, disease, incarceration, rape, lies, betrayal, deceit, etc. We all just got to live knowing one day we'll die hoping our souls will go to Heaven.

"Father please open your gates for P.J. Amen." After I prayed, I sat out in front of the church building crying my heart out.

***

"So, you really leaving?" I asked Arianna who quickly moved around her room gathering her belongings.

"Yes, I love him, sis. Just be happy for me please!" She reached out grabbing a hold of my arm while looking into my eyes.

"I'm telling Uncle Donk," I said yanking away from Arianna.

"Please don't, this is what I've decided. Let me be happy, he makes me happy!"

"Girl, boo you been watching too many movies. This fool done sucked the soul out of you and penetrated your mental. Now you done lost it all. Uncle Donk!" I hollered at the top of my lungs as I headed for the door. "Get off me," I continued as I yanked away from Arianna and shoved her forcefully.

She hit the floor hard as she peered up at me in disbelief. I took off towards Uncle Donk's study. Arianna was tripping and I love her too much to let her do something so foolish.

"Unc?"

"Yes." Uncle Donk sat on the edge of his sofa fiddling with the hairs on his chin.

"Why it's so dark? What you doing, meditating?"

"Kadejah, what is it baby girl?" he asked the frustration was evident.

"Arianna packing her stuff, trying to go move in with this dude."

"What dude?" he asked instantly jumping to his feet. His calm demeanor instantly turned into a menacing scowl.

"A guy she met at work."

"The coffee shop?" he asked in pursuit of her room. Donk pushed open the door, but she was nowhere in sight.

"Arianna! Arianna!" we took turns yelling her name, but it was obvious that she was nowhere in the room.

"She must have run out the front door when I went to go get you."

"Nah, she left through here," Donk spoke with his back to me as he peered out of the slightly ajar window. The curtains blew lightly.

"It's all good I got something for her ass. She thinks she grown, and she knows what's best. How can you know someone you barely met? This guy could be a killer, psych patient, rapist, or anything. Her ignorant ass done ran off with him." I stood there watching Uncle Donk. I felt so bad cause I could only imagine how he felt. First P.J. and now this.

"Yes, I have an emergency. I want to report my sixteen-year-old daughter Arianna Jenkins as a runaway." I listened on as he gave the police a brief description of Arianna. Uncle Donk usually never involved the police, so I was a bit taken aback.

"What?" he asked pausing in mid-stride. "Look I don't trust no niggas around my little girls. I made a vow, I would protect my family at all cost. P.J. is the second that has died on me at the hands of someone else. I wasn't there for Quayo and I wasn't there for P.J. So, since I can't do it alone, I need reinforcements. Motherfuckas who are trained to serve and protect."

"I understand," I agreed peering into his troubled eyes.

He looked so distressed and drained. He kissed me on my fore-head and walked out of the room. I wanted to lift his spirits, but I honestly didn't know what to say. Seconds later I heard the front door slam. I searched for the empty Fila box under my bed and opened the lid, the scent from the expensive weed instantly lit up my room and I hadn't even put fire to it.

Ring! Ring! Ring!

I looked down at Caleb's number on my screen.

"Hello?"

"Let me in," he said.

"Let you in?" I asked confused. "Where you at?"

"Outside your window."

"What?" I ran to the window moved the curtain to the side and there stood Caleb outside my window. I lifted the window as far as it could go and let him in.

"You could've called and told me you were on your way. You just popped up on a bitch."

"I miss you, Kadejah, and I had to see you." He grabbed me by the neck, pulled me closer, and roughly pressed his lips against mine.

His lips were soft. I wanted to push him away, but I wanted it. I needed it. The night I spent with Lil' Tim awoke some things in-side me and since then I'd been having this urge. This itch I can't scratch on my own. Caleb began to ease the shirt over my head. I then took matters into my own hands and quickly peeled my clothes off. He peered at me in bewilderment, but he didn't utter a word. Standing in front of him with just my socks on he looked me up and down in pure satisfaction. He quickly ripped his clothes off and attacked me with his lips. He shoved me on the bed and planted kisses all over my body.

"Please fuck me, Caleb! I been waiting on this," I whispered afraid Uncle Donk might've returned. His pecks ceased as he peered up into my eyes.

"Oh, that's what you want?" he asked with his hands intertwined with mine.

I nodded my head in approval spreading my legs further apart. Caleb buried his head in the nape of my neck while lifting my left leg in the air. He took his penis out of his Hanes boxer briefs and slowly entered my opening one inch at a time.

"Sssss, oooh, Caleb! Hold on!" He ignored my cries and inched further and further before completely shoving himself inside of me.

The forceful thrust caused me to snap my legs shut, but Caleb's strong arms wouldn't allow them to close. He sucked on one of my breasts while slowly working my insides.

"Yo' shit wet and tight," He mumbled, as he leaned to the side hitting me with deep long strokes that made my eyes roll to the back of my head and my breathing to become irregular.

After plunging into my goodies my body became more relaxed and he quickened his pace.

"Ooohhh, this feels so good," I expressed barely able to speak.

"This my pussy, Kadejah?"

"Yes, it's yours. This pussy's forever yours." The moment felt so good I didn't want it to end.

"Turn over." I was so fragile I moved like an old woman. Caleb flipped me on over. I guess I wasn't moving fast enough.

Boom!

"Shit!" I moved Caleb. "That's my uncle you have to go!" I said jumping to my feet.

I moved like a track star. I thought I was drained, guess not. Caleb laid motionless looking confused.

"Get dressed you have to go. My uncle will kill you!"

He smacked his lips before climbing out of the bed. "I'm too grown for this shit," he mentioned quickly getting dressed.

I ran to the door, slowly opened it, and peeked down the hall-way to see if Uncle Donk was coming my way.

"Don't blame me you been knowing my age."

He waved me off then lifted the window. "I'll call you," he said before climbing out.

Soon as Caleb was outside, I watched him jog to his car and peel off. I shut the window and locked it, then laid across my bed and smiled as I thought of the amazing sex while dodging Uncle Donk.

Chapter 22

Bry

I bopped slowly through the house singing Shania's Favorite hymns. She awoke me from a deep slumber wailing as if someone was physically harming her. I made her a warm bottle while attempting to rock her back to sleep, but she was fighting it. Shania didn't sleep much, she was always so busy looking around afraid she would miss something.

"It's nothing going on, NyNy. You can lay down," I teased wiggling the pacifier around inside of her mouth.

She peered up at me and smiled exposing her gums and deep dimples. I carefully stroked her thin black curly hair. She kicked out her chubby legs rapidly until she grew tired and then I laid her on top of the sofa. I peered into her eyes as I thought about her deadbeat father. He was the most dysfunctional bum I'd ever met in my life. When I first met Pierre, he looked and carried himself like the perfect gentlemen. He had a nice 2017 Mercedes Benz, dressed nice, smelled good, and gave me whatever I thought I wanted.

I should've known dude wasn't right when I attended one of his family gatherings and he viciously attacked his brother for staring at me too long. Instead of his trashy ass mother diffusing the situation she cheered Pierre on. I looked on in astonishment before grabbing my purse and calling Uber. They were all so caught up in the drama no one realized I was gone until the next morning. I don't mean shoving and wrestling. They were throwing blow for blow and there was blood. The sight was gruesome. Despite his insane behavior I still stuck around. The sex wasn't great, the fact of the matter is I fell in love with Pierre.

Flaws and all, being that I loved him I owed him loyalty because he had my heart. A minuteman with a four-inch dick didn't make me love him any less. He was my king until the night that madness occurred. At first, he was simply doing the drug, but as time passed the drug begin to do him. I was pregnant with Shania at the time. Pierre had asked me for fifty dollars, but I didn't have it. I was tired of giving him money. He slapped me to the ground and snatched my purse. Little did he know it was just a measly ten dollars inside of the coach bag, I guess once he realized that and he went ballistic. The next morning on Fox 4 Breaking News. His ugly ass appeared on the screen. Apparently, he snatched an eighty-eight-year-old lady's purse at a Valero gas station, but I assumed the elderly lady put up a good fight because he pushed her to the ground unintentionally forcing her to strike her head.

She died three hours after the incident, a blood vessel popped and she bled internally, killing her instantly. He was charged with capital murder anytime there's sexual assault or robbery taken place it's capital murder. He was sentenced to 45 years in state prison.

Ring! Ring! Ring!

"Speaking of the devil," I mumbled looking down at Tonya's name on my screen.

"Hello?"

"What is it, Tonya?"

"No, I cannot take you to South Dallas to get a tattoo. Shania has a cold and I'm not taking her out in this wea—"

Click!

Oh, no she didn't, I thought, looking down at my phone in shock. This bitch just hung up in my face.

Knock! Knock! Knock!

I guess she figured I'd have no choice but to take her if she pops up, I thought. I jumped to my feet and hurried to the door. I was about to let her have it.

"Damn, what's up momma?" Mun asked a bit startled.

"I'm sorry, Mun, I thought you were my annoying mother in law."

"No need to apologize."

I looked him up and down admiring his swag. He wore black Gucci sweatpants, a hoodie with the matching beanie, and a pair of fire-red Air Jordan IV.

"Can I come in?" he asked

"Ooohhh, shit! Where are my manners? Come on in, I'm sorry," I said stepping to the side.

As soon as Mun bypassed a whiff of his Givenchy cologne hit me, stirring up my insides.

"Waahhh! Waahhh!"

"Sshhh! Sshhh!" I picked Nya up and patted her on the back.

"How old is she?"

"Nine months."

"Okay," Mun said rubbing his goatee. He looked like he was thinking about something.

"What's wrong?" I ask.

"Where her daddy?"

"He was sentenced to forty-five years in prison before she was born."

"Damn, so what, he'll see parole in a little over twenty years? Man, I can't even count that high. I know that shit must fuck with him. She's going to be grown by the time he gets out."

"That's his fault, he did some dumb shit."

"Waaahhh! Waahhh!" Shania whined.

"Let me see her," Mun demanded.

He never got up from the sofa. He just held his arms out. I placed her in his arms, and he cradled her close to his chest. He didn't hum or sing. He didn't rock her, yet she didn't make a single sound. For a minute she just peered up at him.

"She's beautiful, ma. What's her name?"

"Shania"

"Shania, you beautiful just like your mother," Mun's comment instantly made me blush.

On the outside, Mun appeared to be the typical thug, but really underneath the designer clothes and dope boy persona, he was the perfect gentlemen.

"Do you have kids?"

"Yes, me and my ex legally adopted my niece."

"Your brother's little girl?"

"Nah, it's a long story momma. It's nothing against you but before I ramble off my personal business to a chick. She has to be mine and before I make you mine I check for certain qualities. I'm not done with my evaluation, ma."

"Oh, okay," I answered a bit taken aback. "I can't be mad, lame bitches make it hard for women like me." I peered over at Shania who was fast asleep. "Let me go lay her down."

"Nah, ma, I don't want her to wake up, she good."

"Oh, okay. You sure?" Honestly, the seat of my panties was soaked, and I was ready to put Shania to bed so I could see what this nigga was really working with.

"You don't have to ask me a second time I'm positive, ma. I didn't come over here to get some pussy. I came to get to know you better. I could've gone anywhere and got some pussy," he responded cockily.

How did he know my mind was on sex? I thought

"Nah, I'm not that type of chick. I saw that she was sleep so I wanted to lay her down."

"Yeah, whatever." He chuckled.

Mun and I laughed and talked for the rest of the night. Shania woke up once or twice but not once did she cry. He was so goofy and outspoken, and I enjoyed every minute of it. I shared more about my baby's father and my upbringing thinking Mun would open up more but he didn't. He just sat there peering at me through those chestnut-brown eyes. His peanut-butter complexion was so smooth it made me want to touch it. Just to see if it was as smooth as it looked.

From time to time he would remove his beanie to massage his scalp. His full and neatly trimmed beard was faded to perfection only complimenting his fresh cut. He rocked a low fro that was tapered on the sides and the back. The way he looked at me made me nervous. Making me cautious of the things I say. His stare was demanding and profound making me feel transparent. I figured it was pointless to lie.

"Okay, let me get going it's late," Mun said looking at his watch.

"What time is it?" I ask standing to my feet.

"Three twenty-five a.m."

"*Three twenty-five a.m.*?" I ask wide-eyed.

Mun leaned up and slowly stood to his feet careful not to wake Shania.

"Waahhh! Waahhh!" she yelled out as soon as he laid her on top of the sofa.

He turned to walk away but I sensed the discomfort in his eyes as he tried to ignore it.

"She'll be okay, I'm going to feed her and put her to bed."

"Waahhh! Waahhh! Waahhh!" He looked torn between the idea of leaving and staying which confused me.

"Fuck it." He surrendered removing his hoodie revealing his crisp white V-neck shirt as he lifted the hoodie over his head, his V-neck inched up exposing a bit of his chiseled midsection. Forcing my mind to wander. He untied his shoes then placed them in the corner of the room. He lifted Shania off the couch, and stretched out on the sofa, placing her directly on his chest.

"I'll just leave early in the morning I have somewhere important to be, but I don't have nothing going on tonight," he assured.

I don't remember if I fell asleep first or not but, I was the first to awake. I looked over at him and Shania who was sleeping peacefully. The sight alone brought tears to my eyes. Since the knowledge of Shania's existence, I wanted a family. I wanted her to be blessed with the presence of both parents unlike most children including myself. Little girls growing up in this era without actual fathers is rough. I didn't say father figure I said a father. See it's less likely for a dad to sexually and verbally harm his own seed rather than a man with no real relation to harm someone else's.

My stepfather raped me several times. I was just a little girl although, he was dating my mom. He didn't give a damn about me. For years I was attracted to older men, my mother couldn't understand it either until I realized I was looking for a daddy. Finding myself with the short end of the stick because I didn't know my worth. I thought if he beat me, he loves me. If he buys me nice things and takes care of me, he loves me. So, if he cheats or causes any form of detriment, I should forgive him and stay because he loves me, but, oh was I wrong. I jumped to my feet, hurried to the restroom, and took a quick shower. I slipped on my cotton candy robe I'd purchased from Victoria Secrets a few months ago. I quietly and quickly prepared breakfast.

I was making Mun maple bacon and sausage, Spinach & avocado Frittata, and blueberry pancakes. I was whipping the eggs when I thought I felt someone watching me. I turned around and spotted Mun standing in the foyer of the kitchen with a wide awake and joyful Shania.

"Oohhh, it smells good in here. Quit acting like you know what you doing, I heard that microwave going," he joked.

"Nothing goes inside the microwave but Shania's bottles."

Mun inched closer invading my space. "Okay do ya' thang chef, Bry. I appreciate you cause I am on E. What time is it?"

"Well, I knew you mentioned waking up early so I tried to have this ready early so you could start your day its six twenty-six."

"Thanks, ma, that's perfect timing."

"No thank you. You didn't have to stay."

"No need to thank me. You didn't force me, neither did she. I wanted to stay."

"When will I see you again?"

"Oh, that's it? You just want to see me?"

I blushed at his comment. "That's not all—"

"Well, tell me what you want," he said inching closer.

He was so close I could feel his breath. I closed my eyes but, when I realized there was no saliva swapping, I quickly opened them. My shoulders sagged in embarrassment when I spotted Mun calmly eating the bacon staring back at me.

"Let me finish making your plate since you're so hungry."

Chapter 23

Shaniece

I applied the final touches of make-up, for hours I watched different Youtube tutorials on eyebrows. It took me nearly two hours to pull them off, but they were on fleek. I needed everything to be perfect, tonight was Twan's and I first official date. We had been conversing for a few days now. The night he gave Persuasia his number, she gave it to me. I texted him pretending he gave me the number himself. Him being the typical nigga went along with it not realizing it was bullshit. There was no telling how many hoes phone he'd put his number in that night. I didn't give a damn I just wanted to be the chosen one.

Knock! Knock! Knock!

Shit! I knocked all my makeup products into the drawer and rushed to the door. I tugged on the sides of the tight-fitted dress from Forever 21. Although my dress was cheap as fuck. It complimented my thigh-high Balenciaga boots. I spent my entire refund check I received from East Field College after I enrolled in school. The money was for my books and tuition, but those boots became first priority at the moment. I figured the expensive boots would keep him from noticing the tacky dress. I smacked my lips as soon as I opened the door and spotted Persuasia.

"Hey to you, too, ho," she said closing the door behind her.

"Heeyyy," I responded in an irritable tone.

"What's wrong, bitch? You ain't happy to see me?"

"Why you got them damn shades on?" I asked yanking them off her eyes.

"I'm good," she lied. Persuasia was high as hell. "Now you know I just buried my son. I have to stay lit when I'm sober all I do is cry."

"Let me make you a drink," I offered before walking away.

"Damn, Shaniece, uh-uh your ass flatter than what I thought," she capped.

I whipped around appalled. "For real, bitch?" I asked cupping my ass cheeks.

"You on no doubt. Beyond beautiful but that ass looks like two pancakes. I'm not talking about the fluffy ones from iHop. The ones you get in the county jail that's made without eggs and milk. Just batter and water.

"Bitch, fuck you." I stormed off, fuck Persuasia, and her opinion.

"Come here! I didn't mean it like that," she said chasing me. "Look just wear your booty pad and once we get him, I'll go half with you on the surgery."

"Mommy makeover?"

"Yeah, I got you," Persuasia agreed.

"Don't be lying with your stuntin' ass."

"I'm not, I'm going to get going and let you finish getting dressed."

"Okay, he should be here at any minute."

"Call me as soon as you get back," she said walking out of the front door.

I rushed to my bedroom and slid on the butt pad.

Twan and I parked in the lot of the Texas Roadhouse. I cut my eyes at him the entire ride. He looked so appeasing.

Persuasia was trippin, I thought, admiring his succulent lips.

His fade alone had me throbbing in between the legs. He was real smooth and laid back. His cappuccino colored skin was flawless. He didn't have a bit of facial hair. His brows were thick, and his lashes were long. His eyes were medium brown, slightly slanted. Although you could stick a penny through his gap, his teeth were straight and remarkably white.

We climbed out of his Audi and walked to the entrance.

"Damn, that ass sitting fat, I got you ma," he said opening the door to the restaurant.

The scene inside was smooth and serene. Quite a few people were in attendance, but no one was waiting to be seated.

"Table for two?" the waitress asked rubber necking past me.

"Yes," Twan answered, he placed his hand on the rear of my back as I led the way to the table.

I was silently praying he didn't inch down any further. I was so nervous I quickened my pace.

"You okay?" he asked as I quickly flopped down in my seat.

"Yes, boo my feet hurt already." He flashed that sexy smile and I almost melted. "I want you to order for me. That'll tell me what type of guy I'm dealing with," I continued.

"Oh, that's not a problem. While we're waiting, tell me a few short, and long-term goals."

"Okay, I'll tell you one of each. One of my short-term goals is to get plastic surgery and my long-term goal is to meet Anthony Davis."

"Huh?" The wrinkles in his forehead displayed his confusion.

"What's wrong?"

"Well, that sounds more like a wish list," he said before chuckling.

"Well, tell me yours."

"My goal is to succeed," he stated, simply.

Twan and I rambled on like we'd known each other forever. I could not eat my food for talking so much. It had been a minute since I vibed with someone the way I did with Twan, but I kept my guard up remembering the task at hand. I knew not to reveal any facts about myself. I'm pretty sure after revealing my goals he thinks I'm dumb as a box of rocks.

He's the idiot if he believes it. If I didn't need the money, I'd really consider taking Twan serious. He wasn't your average dude, nor the average dope boy. It was all temporary. His current lifestyle served one purpose. He wasn't selling drugs to make a living. He was making a living so he wouldn't have to sell drugs. The ringing of his phone ceased our conversation.

"Hello?

"Hell yeah! Well, I mean, I'm a little tied up. How long you going to be?"

"Bet, I'm on my way."

"Look shawty money calling and I got to go get it. I'm only gon be tied up for 'bout an hour. I have to dip off to my spot. I can drop you off or you can dip off with me so we can finish our conversation."

"Sure, I'm cool with that."

Bingo!

A guy stood on the porch talking on the phone when Twan and I pulled up. It was evident he was a bit anxious. For what? I don't know. He was handsome. If Persuasia wasn't so gone behind Donk I'd hook her up.

"I see ya," he said when me and Twan climbed the steps.

He sized me up and I matched his gaze before he flashed a smile.

"I'm about to grab my shit and I'll be right back. I 'preciate you for coming and holding things down. I'm sorry, Ms. Lady for interrupting y'all lovely evening," he said jogging off and hopping into a grey Buick Lacrosse.

I followed Twan inside the almost empty house. A 50-inch plasma sat on top of an empty laundry bin. I watched the traffic from the T.V. screen. There was a camera at the end of the street, the front porch and two more but I couldn't pinpoint where they were at.

"You want something to drink? I got Cranapple, Cranberry and Orange juice."

"Sunny D?"

"Nah, girl the off-brand shit that don't have a brand, so it actually says orange juice."

"You funny, I'll take Cranberry juice."

I peered around the house, it was quite empty. A circular wooden table with four chairs sat in the far corner. Just a small sofa in the middle of the living area. A small lamp rested on top of a cardboard box. I tried looking around to see how the transactions were made, but I couldn't quite figure it out. I could hear Twan rumbling through something in the rear of the house. I just sat there with my legs crossed while waiting for him to return.

My heartbeat sped up when I saw the two guys approaching climbing the steps two at a time. I relaxed a bit when I realized they were crackheads. I rushed to the back to get Twan before they knocked so I could be nosey as well.

"Twan, two guys are about to knock on—"

Ding!

Before I could even finish my sentence. I tried keeping my eyes on Twan but I couldn't help but notice the money and dope in the shoebox on the floor next to him and the small bags of dope in his hand.

"Here this two twenties and two tens serve them if they either one, if not come back. Take this, too." He retrieved the large Glock from his waist.

I was scared as hell, but if this is what I had to do to get closer to him, then so be it.

"Okay," I replied walking to the front door. The doorbell sounded again, and I jumped. "Calm down girl you got this," I said taking a deep breath before slightly opening the door.

"Let me get two tens, man," the fiend said as peered around nervously.

I assumed tens was smaller than twenties so I handed the two smaller rocks after collecting the crumbled twenty-dollar bill. As soon as I dropped the dope in his hand, I slammed the door and locked it.

"You good, shawty?" Twan asked standing behind me.

He wrapped his hands around my waist, placing his chin on my shoulder. The Versace Dylan blue cologne he wore invaded my nostrils instantly. Forcing my clit to thump. I took a deep whiff while he planted soft pecks on my neck.

"Let's finish our conversation before were interrupted again," I suggested.

I handed him the money, dope, and pistol then removed my boots and sat comfortably on the sofa.

"So, how often are you here?"

"Damn near all day, all night and the wee hours of the morning trying to chase that sack."

"You don't have no one to relieve you when you want time off?"

"Yeah, my boy, the one you just saw. We rotate. Me, I don't like off days. I want all the money. I can sit in here twenty-four hours a day, three hundred and sixty-five days a year. I don't get tired."

Me and Twan's conversation advanced to another level when things got personal. I almost slipped up and said something I shouldn't have but I caught myself. He shared secrets, insecurities, and plans for the future. He made me feel so comfortable and welcomed. I could tell he was feeling a bitch cause his tongue was looser than a hooker's pussy, but when that check call those feelings are put on the back burner. I leaned in and pressed my lips against his, I just had to feel them I couldn't contain myself another second.

Ding!

I looked in the direction of the T.V. and saw the guy from earlier standing on the porch.

"He must've left something," Twan said evidently upset.

He stood to his feet and went to unlock the door. Dude didn't look familiar, but he eyed me as if he knew me. Twan flopped down next to me on the couch.

"Look, bae, it's getting late I have to be up at five a.m. We can hook up tomorrow," I informed.

He smacked his lips before responding, "Yeah, come on." He started rubbing his waves forward.

I could tell Twan was a bit upset cause he wanted a taste of this voodoo. I gave my pussy that nickname a while back. I had to get a restraining order on this dude I used to date. He claimed I put something in his food which I found awkward because I never cooked for him. The truth is I didn't know how to cook. I put this pussy on him and since then he been under my spell. Besides, I had all the information on Twan I needed. Mission complete.

Twan dropped me off at the front of my apartment complex. I claimed to have forgotten my access card so he wouldn't know exactly where I live.

"Where you at?" I anxiously asked Persuasia.

"I'm at the crib. I'm not feeling the club tonight."

"Okay, well, feel this, I got everything you need to know 'bout Twan."

"I'm on my way."

I reclined onto the worn-out sofa. I was so anxious, I couldn't close my eyes. I glanced around the small and cluttered living room. A few roaches crawled behind the cheap paintings. I purchased from the thrift store down the street. My neighbors on both sides were nasty as hell so, in spite of the fact, I cleaned and bleached my spot. Everyday roaches found a way into my home. I don't watch T.V. but I have a nice 42-inch plasma. It's not huge but it's mine. It's placed on a black stand I purchased from Walmart, the instructions were beyond difficult, so I threw them away and put it together on my own. The next day I awoke to a loud noise. My plasma had fallen, screen first. When I picked it up and inspected it, it looked perfectly fine until I turned it on and realized the entire left side was pitch black. That's the reason I don't watch T.V.

I took the initiative to paint the walls in my living room black, to later find out I'd be fined once my lease was up. Shit, I didn't understand the problem. White is too bland, black is festive. I'm tired of being broke, merely existing.

Knock! Knock! Knock!

The knock on the door snapped me out of my thoughts. I rushed to the door nearly tripping over my own two feet in the process.

"What's wrong with you?" Persuasia asked as soon as I swung the door open.

"Nothing, I'm good. Why?"

"Just asking," she said closing the door behind her.

"Okay, what you got?"

"He sells dope, he g—"

"Is he a worker or boss?" Persuasia chimed in.

"I don't know, he rotates shifts."

"He's a worker."

"It could also mean he's short a worker," I commented

"The possibility of that is slim to none, but okay finish."

"The spot's on Military right there on Brewster street. I even know where he keeps the drugs and money. His shift is seven a.m. to seven p.m. He works every day, sometimes he goes in early."

"Brewster? Do you know the dude's name he works with?"

"No, I saw him but I don't know him. Twan never said his name."

"Is the house black and white?" Persuasia pried.

"Yes!"

"What the fuck, Twan works for Donk?"

"No, wait! How do you know it's Donk's spot?"

"I know my nigga's shit!" she spoke aggressively.

"Bi—" I stopped abruptly noticing the look on her face it was no way in hell she would rob Donk.

"So, that's a no go?" I asked.

"Hell yeah, that's a no go!"

I flopped down on the sofa next to Persuasia. I was a bit upset. Honestly, I didn't blame her, I wouldn't allow anyone to fuck over or fuck with my people. No good.

"I got another one for you, though. This dude is Bossman status."

I listened to Persuasia inform me on this new guy and the role I would play. I didn't give a damn what I had to do. I needed some loot and I needed it now. As soon as the plan was orchestrated, Persuasia gathered her things and left. As soon as I closed the door I rushed to my phone and called Bry.

"Where you at?"

"Sitting at home."

"You got Shania or does Aunt Joyce have her?"

"I have her. Why?" she asked.

"Okay, well, we can get Q to watch her for thirty minutes. I got a lick and it's legit. Swing by now."

Click!

I knew Bry would be here in no time. She only stayed a few minutes away. I didn't mention Twan or Donk's name cause Bry is too loyal. Off the strength of Persuasia, she wouldn't allow me to do something so absurd. But I couldn't let this one go. Persuasia had opened my eyes to something I wouldn't have thought to do myself.

I chain-smoked the Newports until I heard Bry's soft knock at the door.

"Hey, Niecy Pooh!" I yelled while closing the door behind me.

Shania looked up at me. Her huge bedroom eyes glistened as she sucked on the pacifier. Bry had her wrapped up in what seemed to be a thousand blankets, only exposing her tiny head.

"This better be good," Bry chimed in impatiently

"Look the lick is at a trap, but I know who all in there and exactly where the money is," I informed.

"A trap? Girl, hell nah. You smoking?

"Come on, Bry, it's easy!"

"No! Bitch, don't you see my nine-month-old baby?"

"What if I told you it's twenty gees or more."

"You lying," she spoke looking at me in disbelief.

"On Nya," I swore.

She dropped her head reconsidering the idea. "Okay, if we're going to do this, were going to need Q."

Ah'Million

Chapter 24

Arianna

I knew once Uncle Donk and Kadejah found out about my sweet escape they wouldn't be too pleased. Leaving Quincy wasn't an option. With Uncle Donk I may have wanted for nothing, with Quincy, I got that *and* a lot of love and affection. He even promised more if I agreed to move in.

I raced down the street with just over-sized Louis Vuitton purse filled with underclothes, hygiene products, my favorite picture of me, PJ, and Kadejah, an outfit or two, and some money I saved from working at the coffee shop. Out of breath, I stopped and quickly phoned Quincy.

"Hello?" he answered

"Bae, I just left, I'm two blocks away from my house."

"Okay, I'm on my way."

Quincy must've been parked somewhere close by because he bent the corner in just a matter of seconds. As soon as he pulled to the curb, I ran to the car and hopped in. A short while later, we were at his house.

"You're eighteen I don't understand why your uncle would trip?" Quincy said dropping his keys onto the kitchen table.

"He's just overprotective. You know how men are with their little girls," I responded flopping down on the sofa. I was exhausted.

"You not that tired. Get your sweaty ass off my couch and go shower."

"I am, I'm just t—" Quincy inched closer gazing at me through the most callous set of eyes.

His rude demand caught me off guard without another word spoken. I flew to the shower. My phone rang non-stop since the moment I jumped in the car with Quincy. It saddened my spirit to look at Uncle Donk's name flash across my screen.

Relaxed in the tub of hot water I imagined myself in a different world around different people under different circumstances. I then heard a loud knock at the door. Forcing me to jump but I settled down after reflecting on Quincy's conversation in the car. Whoever he was talking to on the phone, they were on their way over.

Boom! Boom! Boom!

I nearly jumped out of my skin that time. This wasn't a love tap or a friendly knock. It was more of an open up now knock. Which I found disbelieving cause Quincy wasn't the thuggish type.

My concerns were answered moments later when I heard, "Police, open up!"

I looked from left to right as if I'd find an escape but found nothing. I hopped out of the tub slipping and sliding on the tile floor trying to grab a hold of whatever to keep from falling.

"Excuse me, ma'am. Get dressed and step out now," the cop ordered as he stood on the other side of the door.

What the hell I do? I thought. "Yes, sir" I answered.

Completely dumbfounded I quickly got dressed and glanced in the mirror. I opened the door and there stood two male officers one of them held a pair of cuffs.

"Turn around and place your arms behind your back," he demanded.

"Why am I being arrested?" I asked as I felt the tears quickly filled my eyes.

He read me my rights and walked me through Quincy's home.

"Once we thoroughly investigate, if we find out you knew this young lady or had any dealings with her you will face charges," the officer announced on the way out.

I knew Quincy was fuming on the inside after finding out my age in such a dangerous way. If only they'd turn their heads for a split second he'd reach out and choke me after I led him to believe I was eighteen years old. At that moment I wished I could call Uncle Donk to save me, but I was pretty sure it would take more than him to get me out of this mess.

Chapter 25

Kadejah

I was still distraught about the jewels Caleb dropped on me about Tru's sentence. First, I was upset with Tru for lying to me but then I put myself in her situation. If I had a life sentence and fell in love with someone with little to no time, what other way could I convince her to stick around? Honesty doesn't always help the situation. I'm pretty sure I wasn't the only female she fell in love with, maybe she tried the honesty thing once before and it didn't work so she chose a different route.

Since finding out I been working non-stop to help her out of her situation. From appeal attorneys to parole and Habeaus Corpus attorneys. I've concluded that it's a process and nothing is going to happen overnight. Little does Tru know, I would've never left her side if she had 100 years. My loyalty don't blow like the wind it's planted and stiff like cement.

"Hey, Tru," I greeted cheerfully once I spotted her standing beside the visiting room.

A huge smile spread across her face as soon as she heard my voice.

"Come on." She motioned me inside we quickly sat down and reached across the table to hold hands while waiting for the officer to close the doors.

I was glad Tru picked the room the furthest down the hall. We stared into each other eyes with similar thoughts. Thought of instant intimacy as soon as the door is shut and the officer walks away.

"Hey, be careful leaving I saw Mr. Woods coming in while you were out in the lobby."

"Okay, hopefully, he don't make his way down here," I said pretending to be concerned.

Woods was the last person I was afraid of at this point. If only Tru knew, I rode with Woods. As soon as the C.O. left Tru and I leaned over the table and attacked each other with our lips. I wrapped my arms around her neck, and she grabbed me by my cheeks. Moans and grunts escaped our mouths turning me on even more.

"Okay, okay, Kadejah," Tru mumbled while backing away.

"You just don't know how much I miss you, Tru," I admitted taking a seat.

"I miss you, too, baby. How you been?"

"I'm okay, I'm maintaining. My sister came home today. Speaking of my sister did you know her?"

"What's her name? I remember you said it starts with an A."

"Arianna."

"Arianna, Arianna," Tru repeated peering down at the table in deep thought.

"How she look, bae?" She continued looking dumbfounded.

"She's medium brown, nice coal-black, curly hair and she's petite."

"Nah, I don't think I know her," Tru answered.

"It's funny you say that because when I asked her if she knew you she told me she introduced herself to you and y'all spoke whenever y'all were in passing," I stated.

"I—I been so distraught my memory been shot bu—but if you can send a picture, it'll refresh my memory," Tru uttered.

My heart saddened as I thought about Tru's future and the mental anguish she struggled with daily. To hear the word *life* your natural reaction is, I'll never see daylight. Not knowing in seemingly hopeless situations you have to keep an optimistic perspective. Relationships may be irreparable, but it's 100 ways to beat the system. Whether you're innocent or guilty.

"You're right it doesn't matter anyways. The only thing that matters is you." Tru began sobbing uncontrollably as I calmed her down.

I peered at her, dumbfounded by the sudden reaction.

"Kadejah—I—I have t—to tell you something," she spoke through sniffles.

"What is it, bae? Tell me" I urged.

"Promise me you won't leave."

"I haven't left yet. Spit it out before our time is up."

172

"I have a life sentence," she confessed.

I pretended to act as if the news was shocking and fresh, gasping as I placed my hand over my heart. I cried all over again like I did when I heard the news from Caleb.

"Oh, my that's a long time Tru."

"I understand," she responded dropping her head.

"Oh, don't say it like that. I'm gon' hold you down until the day I go. But I can't tell you I'm going to put my life on hold, Tru."

"That's the last thing I want you to do momma."

"Well, what's the first thing you want me to do?"

"Just remain loyal to me, and only me."

I informed Persuasia on my whereabouts once I found out Caleb couldn't take me home. I definitely didn't want a repeat of last time when I decided to find my own way home. Uncle Donk had been unusually quiet around the house. Since Arianna had been home, she acted distant and was jumpy most of the time.

Although, I felt played I wanted to be in Lil' Tim's presence. He texted me twice last night trying to take me out, but I ignored him and went to bed.

Honk! Honk!

I darted to Persuasia's Chevy Malibu that was parked in the middle of the lot.

"Hey!" she greeted.

"Hey, P, thanks for the ride."

"Anytime. You have a good visit?"

"Yes, Lawd," I joked making Persuasia laugh. She swerved out the lot and before veering onto I-35 I said, "Take me to Lil' Tim's."

Ah'Million

Chapter 26

Mun

Bry and I strolled through NorthPark mall laughing and stealing glances at each other. When I was around Bry it was as if nothing mattered at that moment. I was planning to fall back cause honestly. I felt myself falling and I refused to trust another bitch with my heart. I was even becoming attached to her seed. The shit was wild.

"Hey, let's stop here," she suggested.

We'd been in the mall for nearly an hour now. Once I get Bry where I want her, I'll give her cash and let her splurge, but I won't accompany her to a mall, flea market, or anything similar ever again.

"I want this one, bae. Isn't it cute?" she asked holding up the mini Hermes bag.

"I guess, you can't put shit in it," I responded peering around. "What that tag say?" I asked curiously.

"Twenty-eight hundred."

"*Twenty-eight hundred?* All you can fit in that bitch is a lipstick. That's a lot of money for something so useless," I commented.

Bry poked her lip out and placed the bag back on the rack.

"Ma, just because it's not worth it in my eyes, doesn't mean you're not going to get it. You want it, I'm gon' buy it. It's about you, get that Louis Vuitton one right there for Nya."

"Aww thanks, bae. I love you!" she voiced loudly wrapping her arms around my neck.

You don't love me, you love what I do for you, I thought.

I paid for the bags and we circled the mall once again before leaving.

"Fam, fam!"

"Huh?"

"Damn, nigga what's on ya mind?"

"Nothing, Arianna back home I been keeping a close eye on her."

"Yeah, cause if I see that nigga I'm gon' kill him."

"Hey, this number in Trigga's phone matches the number the older guy gave us. So, this bitch must've paid both of them."

"What? Are you serious?" I asked appalled by his discovery.

"Look." Donk stood showing me the number on both screens.

"Call ya boy Jeff."

"Damn, Fam I forgot to tell you Jeff's dead. They found him on a cruise ship slumped face down in a plate of spaghetti."

"Word?"

"On Quaylo," Donk swore.

"I got a new guy his name's Bruce. He isn't as swift but he pretty good. Hold on." Donk dialed the number on his phone before placing it up to his ear. "Hey, if I give you a number how long will it take for you to locate the person?" he asked Bruce.

"Bet! The number two-one-four-eight-six-one-seven-zero-two-eight," he voiced before disconnecting the call.

"What he say?" I asked.

"If it's an iPhone it'll take no more than three minutes anything other than that will take about fifteen."

"Let's hope the bitch team iPhone."

"You strapped?" Donk asked.

"At all times," I shot back.

"Bet, let me grab my shit. As soon as he chimed in with an address we out." Donk took off to his study as I reclined on the sofa.

Bing!

I hurried and snatched the phone from the table, opening the message.

"Yes! Donk, let's go!"

"Hey, this address familiar to you or you want me to put it in the GPS?" I asked jogging to my Dodge Challenger that was parked in the driveway.

"Six-two-four-two Seco? Seco is the street across from the lake June Transition center."

"Sure is." Slamming the doors shut I push start the whip and turned the volume up on *Gucci Mane's* latest hit *Bipolar* before peeling off.

Hours had passed, but there was no sign of Mariyah. I spotted a few young dudes exit the house an hour ago. However, I didn't think too heavily on the idea of approaching them. We didn't need any unnecessary blood on our hands.

"Man, I'm getting hungry fam," I announced slouching further into my seat.

"Let me see your phone," Donk said. I handed him the phone while peering into the direction of the house.

"Hey, Tim, where you at?"

"Do you have Mariyah as a friend on Facebook or Instagram?"

"Okay, screenshot me a recent picture of her."

"Don't worry 'bout what's going on. Me and Mun got it, just find me a picture," Donk voiced loudly before hanging up.

"What's the plan?" I asked.

"We wait."

"Okay, wake me up when something pops off," I said closing his eyes.

I didn't think he was serious until I noticed how silent the car became. I twirled the .380 around my fingers while peering out of the window. Thoughts of my sister and mother flooded my mind.

"Fam, I'm sick of this life," Donk blurted out.

"Huh? What happened!" I jumped, looking startled wiping the drool from the side of his mouth.

"Nigga chill out," I said. "I'm sick of this life," Donk repeated calmly.

"Why you say that?" I asked leaning up.

"We doing the same shit now that we was doing before momma died."

It's always something with this street shit. Look at us, look where we at and what we're about to do. Yeah, it's for a good cause, but at the same time, this shit gots to eventually end.

"I agree." I nodded my head slowly rubbing my chin hair.
Bing!
My eyes quickly diverted to the phone.
"Aww, mane! Look at this bullshit!" I couldn't believe my eyes as I turned the screen toward Donk so he could get a glance of the incredulous sight.
"You can't be serious," he expressed matching my gaze.
"All this motherfucking time we been watching this lil' nigga. I mean bitch go in and out this crib and, it's her the whole time," I voiced shaking my head.
"Fuck. We should've had our shit tight. We slipping, what if she would've got at us first? We wouldn't have ever seen it coming." I peered at the screen a second time.
The beauty that trapped Lil' Tim several months ago had completely transformed. Meech's little sister looked more like his little brother. Her long hair was faded, and her tight clothes were replaced with baggy ones. Exposing the Ethika boxer briefs. Her once nude arms were covered in ink, and her strut wasn't the least appeasing due to the added masculinity.
"Well, now, it's no telling when she'll return since she just left," Donk said looking towards the house.
"You right, let's just come back later. It won't be a problem finding this bitch now."

Chapter 27

Bubba

Back to the basics, the only difference was my dawg was gone. I sat on the sofa surfing through the channels at little to no volume. Only forty dollars to my name, I decided to go to the candy house. The candy house was just around the corner. They sold everything, nickel and dime sacks of weed, tunechi, cigarillos, cigarettes, burgers, links, wing baskets, nachos, and all sorts of sodas, candy, and chips.

"Where you going, Bubba?" My mother asked peeking her head around the kitchen.

"The candy house," I replied unlocking the locks.

I was tired of her questioning my every move. Since P.J.'s death, I hadn't been able to shit in peace without her asking me where I'm going. I understand she's worried but, damn. P.J. would be pissed if he was here. We both just knew everything with Rah would go smoothly, but it didn't.

"I can just drive you around there," she offered while drying the dish.

"Nah, mama, I'm good. I'll be back in ten minutes."

She scurried toward me wrapping her arms around my waist.

"Okay! I love you, Hunny, hurry back."

Slightly annoyed I kissed my mother on the forehead and walked out. I zipped up my Givenchy jacket and proceeded down the steps. It was quite chilly but I could see the sun peeking around the cloud. It was still early so the streets were quiet. I walked at a nice pace not wanting my mother to panic. She will hop in her car and come after me if I take too long. As I walked down the alleyway, I couldn't help but notice the opportunity. The unattended and opened cars. The houses with the garages up and the garage doors leading to the inside, wide open. Who's to say that's probably a trap, too. I discreetly shook my head in disbelief as I continue to mob to the candy house.

It's crazy how shit finds you when you're not looking for it, but when are looking for it, it's nowhere to be found, I thought.

Usually, it was a little commotion going on around the candy house but not today. The gray trash bin was knocked over, and a few beer bottles laid in the grass.

Knock! Knock! Knock!

"I haven't seen you in a few days," Ms. Mabel commented, flashing her beautiful teeth.

She wore a floral housecoat and fluffy pink house shoes. Ms. Mabel was the Big Momma of the hood, she was gangsta, too. Everyone respected and loved her. The dope boys, fiends, prostitutes, jack boys, and the eccentric cause she showed love.

"I know Ms. Mabel I been stressing."

"Stressing about what?" she asked staring at me.

"Death of a close friend." Although she knew P.J. I didn't want to say his name. Every time I spoke his name, I relived that moment. A moment I'd never forget.

"What you come to get, son?"

"Two singles, two cigarillos, and a nick."

"*A nick?* Damn, you must not be doing too well, son?" She peered up, over her glasses that rested on the bridge of her nose.

"Somethin'—like that."

"Give me six dollars, the cigarillos on the house," she said.

"Thank you, Ms. Mabel."

"Look, son, to have life is a blessing. Appreciate everyone and everything in it while you can cuz' everybody not able. Go get you a job and get off these streets. The money a little slow but it's consistent and it's yours."

"You right, gangsta," I agreed handing her the ten-dollar bill.

"Don't just agree, do something 'bout it—" she paused looking me into the eyes. She shoved the four dollars into my hand and said, "Alright, we'll see."

I been trying to contact Donk all day yesterday, but I couldn't reach him. I tried making the weed I had stretch but if I would've rolled the blunts any smaller, they would've been skimps. I took it upon myself to pop up at the coffee shop hoping he'd be there. I'd always had a hustler's ambition, but I felt like that bullet P.J. took was intended for me. So, I'd decided to do something different before becoming another statistic.

Bing!

I stepped inside the Subdued and Chic coffee shop. It's a bit fancier than what I expected but I didn't allow it to slow my stride. I spotted the chick at the register who looked to be P.J.'s sister.

Something with an A, I can't remember, I thought.

"Aren't you my brother's friend?" she asked with a puzzled expression on her face. P.J. kept Trigga and I away from his sisters, I don't blame him.

"Yeah, Bubba." I smiled nervously.

"Hi, I'm Arianna. What would you like to order?"

"Oh, nothing, the only caffeine I drink is soda. I'm looking for Donk."

"He's busy, I don't mean to pry but is it something I can help you with? He isn't here, hardly ever is."

"Well, maybe with one of the issues. I remember P.J. telling me he worked here. So, I was hoping to see if I could have his spot?

"Okay, we do have a spot that needs to be filled. But why?" she asked sizing me up. I knew she was eyeing my fly get up.

"Shawty, look I'm down on my nuts. I'm living off hope," I replied shoving my hands in my pocket, as I looked down at the freshly waxed floor. I really missed P.J. he was always ready to ride.

"Stay right here I'm going to make a call real quick."

I looked around while waiting on Arianna to return.

"Hey, Bubba, he said for sho' you can start tomorrow. If you like you can hang around today so you can see how it is."

I scratched the back of my head while gazing around. I really didn't have anything better to do.

"Okay, I'll hang out for another hour, I guess."

"Okay, follow me so I can introduce you to the baker. Amy is also an employee here but she's off," Arianna voiced cheerfully.

"This is Dan. Dan this is Bubba he starts tomorrow."

"Nice to meet you, young blood," Dan stated gripping Bubba's shoulder before walking away.

"Nice to meet you, too," Bubba called out.

Dan had already retreated to his workstation, he wasn't social at all that's what I liked about him.

"So, how you been coping since the death?" Bubba asked.

"It's not easy I just try to stay busy, so I won't have to think about it too much. Uncle Donk isn't the same. He's always gone or not in the mood. Me running away has played a big part in his change of attitude as well. What about you?"

"I just been trying to promote my music. P.J. hooked me up with this big producer who fucked me over. So, I been trying to go about it a different way."

"Have you put it on Spotify or Soundcloud?"

"Soundcloud, but I never heard of Spotify."

"Where you been? Everybody on there."

Ring! Ring! Ring!

Rah's name flashed across my screen as I peered down at my phone. This was the 10th time he called today. I declined it and diverted my attention back to Arianna. We walked back to the front after she gave me a tour of the office seeing P.J.'s mini set up brought tears to my eyes. I sat down at the table closest to the entrance. Using the plastic spoon, I made a beat and begin to flow bobbing my head as the words flowed easily. The scenery outside of the coffee shop coaxed me to go harder. I was so caught up I didn't realize Arianna was sitting beside me.

"Hey, are you going to get that?" she asked eyeing my phone.

"Nah," I replied quickly, I knew it was only Rah with more threats. His threats didn't move me not even a little. If he popped out on me, I was just going to show him what I excelled at other than rap.

Oh, shit my blunt, I thought.

"Look, Arianna what time I need to be here tomorrow?" I ask standing to my feet.

"Six."

"Six in the evening?" I ask shocked.

"No crazy six a.m."

"Damn, that's early, but okay I'll see you then."

182

"See you then!" she yelled from the table.

I posted up a block away from the coffee shop and rolled up the sticky. I couldn't wait to take a toke of the fiya as licked the cigarillo down to perfection. I retrieved the lighter from my pocket and lifted the blunt to my lips, but before I could put fire to it the perfectly rolled blunt went crashing onto the concrete.

"What th—" I looked up and locked eyes with Rah and two more guys.

"So, you ignoring my calls?" Rah inquired standing in front of the two men.

"What it look like? You can answer that for yourself," I shot back.

"Smartass, I see you've put some of your music on Soundcloud?"

"Okay, what's that supposed to mean?"

"You signed a contract fool. That's all your music and rights."

"Fuck you and that contract."

Rah gave one of his men the famous head gesture. I snatched the burner from my waist the same time dude grabbed his. I hated I wasn't in my neck of the wood. I didn't know any short cuts, alleys or anything.

Boom! Boom! Boom! Boom!

He fired shots and so did I, both of us barely missing. By this time the other dude start bussing, too. I scurried behind the waste management dumpster, but not before I was hit in the calf.

"Fuck!" I hollered.

The gun wound slowed me down, It felt like someone was lighting fire to an open wound. I sat on my ass breathing heavily behind the stinky dumpster. I slowly eased my way off the ground using the dumpster for leverage. I peeked around the dumpster once the shooting ceased.

Boom! Boom! Boom!

Feeling the bullet whizz past my nose I instantly stepped back. *Damn, how am I going to do this?* I thought.

Remembering I had my phone in my pocket I called Donk. Shots continue to ring out as I waited anxiously for Donk to answer.

"Come on Donk please answer for me man."

My luck, it went to voicemail. I ended the call and called my mother, the last person I wanted to call. I had no choice, knowing that she'd panic once she heard the gunshots.

"Hello, Bubba, where are you? What is that noise?"

"Ma, sshhh, listen."

"Don't ssshh me. Where are you?"

"Mama, listen, I'm on Buckner behind the Taco Bueno. I need you to come get me now!"

"Aww, baby! Okay, okay, I'm on my way. Hold on, stay on this phone, Bubba."

"Aarrgghh! Okay, ma," I spoke in a low tone wincing from the pain in my leg.

I peeked around the dumpster again to see if the men had moved but, every time I would do so another multiple of shots would fire off in my direction. I gripped my calf applying pressure to the wound. I was losing a lot of blood fast.

"Bubba! Bubba!"

"Mama, quit all that hollering I'm here," I mumbled.

I tightened every muscle in my body to endure the pain, but it was only helping so much. The shooting ceased so I peeked again only this time I only saw two men instead of three. I quickly turned around only to be met by the barrel of a gun. I shook my head in silence staring in the eyes of my maker.

"Bubba, baby answer me!"

"Ma—mama I, I love you," I blurted out before it was too late. *Boom! Boom! Boom!*

Chapter 28

Donk

I sat in my study watching the footage from the robbery. Luckily, a fiend I'd been knowing for a long time happen to stop by the spot to score when he caught a glimpse of the heinous scene. The ajar door granted him access inside the spot to witness everything.

He ran inside, retrieved the tape, and sold it to me for fifty dollars, and fled before the cops arrived, claiming the money and dope had vanished as well. I was tired of burying my people. As well as the betrayal, lies, and mental anguish. I hadn't said more than three words to Arianna since she'd been released. I was so upset with her choices it was best I remained quiet until I was calm enough to converse.

I could tell she felt uneasy being in my presence unable to decipher my mood and thoughts. Keeping her on edge was fine with me.

"Hello?" Mun answered.

"What's up, Bro? Where you at?" I asked.

"Just left Bry's."

"Pull up on me I got something for you." I ended the call, then sat on the sofa.

The expensive weed was the only thing that temporarily eased my mind. I didn't like the girls to see me so distressed especially Kadejah. Luckily, she was gone to visit a friend. I made a mental note to see who this friend was because twice a week around the same time she leaves. I jumped at the sight of Mun's shadow.

"I scared you?" he asked grinning.

"Fuck you, come on." I led the way through the house.

"Here put this on?"

"The fuck? You got the corona?" Mun inquired before putting the face mask on. I opened the door to the basement and walked lightly down the steps.

"Damn, where she come from?" Mun asked through wide eyes as he gazed at a pitiful Mariyah.

The confident and cheerful attitude was gone. She looked timid and frightened tied to the wooden chair. Everything about her appearance was raunchy.

"What that—"

"Shit and piss, she did that as soon as I begin to question her scary ass. It's hard to believe she knows nothing," Donk answered.

"How did you—"

"I ran across her earlier, this morning. Bubba is dead, I received a call from his mother and after consoling her the best way I knew how. I spotted Mariyah going inside the burger shop on Lake June."

"Hold up Bubba is dead? P.J.'s friend? What happened?"

"I don't know. Bubba's mother said he called her in the midst of the shooting to come pick him up. He only mentioned his location. Then it got quiet, he mumbled the words, *I love you* and more shots was fired, this time the shots were loud. She could tell the gunmen was close. By the time she arrived police were all over the place, retrieving Bubba's body from behind the dumpster, placing him on the gurney."

"What the fuck? Damn, I know momma going through it. I'm not good with words, but I'll send her flowers once I leave here," Mun confirmed.

"I was with Bry before you called. I thought I saw the chick that hit our spot. But I didn't know for sure, I was certain it was, though."

"It's all good we going to find that bitch. Speaking of that, you know we took a major hit, huh? I had just copped them bricks."

"Yeah, the usual right?"

"Nah, he made me a deal I couldn't refuse."

"What was that?"

"Cop ten more than the usual and he'll take two-thousand off each one."

"What? Damn, that's gon' hurt us," Mun complained.

"Yeah, it did, big time."

"What's the plan?"

"The stash is nearly empty."

"So, what we looking at Donk?" I stared back at Mun while shaking my head.

"Damn, it's that bad?"

"Fam, it's bad. I put nearly my whole savings into that investment knowing I was going to get it back plus some. Altogether I have a little over two racks and two ounces of glass," I confessed.

"Aww, man, all my Fetti was in the pot. I was leaning on the profit. I been buying mother, daughter Berkin bags, and shit. I got about five gees put up, nothing more!"

"Okay, we got to make somethin' shake, after we finish this." I ripped the piece of duct tape off Mariyah's mouth.

"Aaagghhh!" she hollered out in pain. She dropped her head in defeat seeing that she was in a hopeless situation.

"What was your motive? Why did you kill P.J.?

"Same reason you killed my brother," she mumbled.

"So, leaving Lil' Tim in your basement for dead wasn't enough?"

"Lil' Tim isn't the one I wanted. I wanted you. Got to do what you got to do to get what you want to get."

"Oh, you wanted me shawty?" I grinned.

"Yeah, and I almost had you, but greed gets the best of us."

"What you mean by that?"

"You'll let me live if I tell you?"

"Depends on how valuable the information is."

"I think it's very valuable. Don't you want to know the op in your circle?"

"The op?"

"Yeah, that's what I said, right?"

"Okay, you have my word," I agreed.

"Well, I made a deal your boy couldn't refuse."

"Quit speaking in riddles," Mun chimed in.

She smacked her lips while peering around the empty basement.

"Come on. Who is it?" Donk asked sounding concerned.

"You gon' kill me?" she asked the quivering of her lips expressed her fears.

"I told you, you have my word."

"Lil' Tim, I showed up at the hospital once he was rescued ready to get rid of him for good. When I thought of the perfect idea which was to help me get you or someone close. Which was PJ."

"Why should I believe you?" Mun intervened.

"How do I know the actual shooter behind Meech's death. Wasn't it three of you in my home? I wasn't there, Lil Tim told me."

I fiddled with the hairs on my chin out of pure frustration. I didn't want to believe this chick, but she had a valid point.

"What you think, Lil' bro?" Mun mumbled.

"I don't—"

"Didn't you give my brother the option to die and his family would be good?" she spoke through clenched teeth as the tears fell silently.

I rolled my eyes at the facts she just blurted out. I couldn't believe another snake had been exposed. The pain was evident. Lil' Tim wasn't just another guy I was associated with, he was family. The treachery hit me hard, and it cut deep into my soul.

"Is she right, Fam?" Mun asked looking from me to Mariyah confused.

"She's right, Fam." I sighed.

"Who the fuck these motherfuckas think they playing with? I've got niggas burning us, bitches burning us. They think it's some sweet!" Mun hollered slamming his fist down onto the table.

"Since the day I met Lil' Tim I was nothing but good to him."

"Come on let's go," I demanded standing to my feet.

"Wait!" Mariyah called out.

"Hey, we going to let her live? You don't think she heard too much?" Mun asked trailing close behind.

"Of course not, I forgot about her," Donk said turning around.

I removed the 9mm from his waist and quickly fired two bullets into the side of her face inches above her temple.

Chapter 29

Mun

We parked outside of Tim's apartment and waited in the nearly empty lot. Nearly thirty minutes had passed but neither of us made a move.

"You know I thought Tim was different. I really trusted that young nigga," Donk spoke a little above a whisper.

I could tell he truly cared for Tim, never in my thirty years had I seen him hesitate when carrying out a hit.

"Tim is different, but he's still quite young. You already know when you're young you have to bump your head a few times. The only difference is, the code is something you don't break."

Without responding Donk hopped out and headed up the stairs. I followed closely behind him while he rushed up the stairs two at a time. I lightly shoved Donk to the side while softly knocking on Tim's door. I didn't want the loud knock to alert him.

"What the—what's up, niggas?!" Tim yelled enthused.

"What up, boy," Donk and I replied in unison stepping inside the apartment.

I could tell Lil' Tim picked up on Donk's uneasiness but remained silent. Two plates covered the table which instantly made me shoot a quick look around the place making sure he was alone.

"You good?" Donk asked Tim.

Dressed in just a muscle shirt and basketball shorts, Lil' Tim cheerfully rambled on about old times and how joyful he felt to see us.

"Aye, Tim—" Donk interrupted.

"Look I need to holler at you about something," Donk continued as Tim dropped his head in defeat.

"Look listen let me explain," Tim spoke up.

"You should've been done that," Donk protested.

In one swift motion, he removed the 9mm, pressed the barrel against his forehead, and fired off two shots.

Psst! Psst!

His body dropped like a sack of potatoes. I crossed over his body to take care of the chick. Faintly singing R & B lyrics Donk and I burst inside, but Kadejah was the last person I expected to see reclined against the tub.

"Aagghhh!" she yelled covering her breasts.

I quickly lowered the gun punching a hole in the wall behind me.

"Kadejah, what are you doing here?" Donk ask distraught while we both looked at the wall in the opposite direction. Donk's voice quivered as he spoke.

"What wrong with me being here? I can't chill with Tim?"

Donk's trembling hands could barely hold the gun. "How you get here?"

"Uber, what's the problem? What's with the guns?"

"Don't worry about it just get dressed and let's go," Donk demanded.

"I don't want to leave y'all. Me and Lil Tim chilling."

"Nah, not anymore."

"What's the problem now?"

"He's not responsive, that's the problem."

"He's not what?'

"He's dead!"

"*Dead?* Oh my God. You were that keen on us not being together?" she yelled.

I scowled while peering at her through narrow slits. "*Not being together?* What, you and Tim were a couple?"

"We were working on it and trying to figure out how to tell y'all."

"You not hooking up with the op, he's a sellout. Let's go," I ordered as Donk and I exited the restroom giving Kadejah privacy to get dressed.

"Nooooo!" she wailed once she exited the restroom as she stood in the hallway outside of the bathroom door and spotted Tim's lifeless body sprawled out on the carpet

"Come on, Kadejah," Donk urged.

"Why you do it, Unc?" she asked with tear-stained cheeks.

"It's all part of the game, baby girl," Donk convinced before tightening his lips and shrugging his shoulders.

Tears slowly fell down his smooth, chocolate face as he locked eyes with Kadejah. She buried her face inside her hands and cried like a baby. I stood off to the side in complete silence with my hands buried deep in the pockets of my pants. I hated to see Kadejah so hurt, but she would never understand.

"We have to go," I spoke calmly.

I scooped a distraught Kadejah off her feet, cradled her in my arms, and exited Tim's apartment.

Ah'Million

Chapter 30

Persuasia

I been blowing up his phone since the night before trying to get him on my line, but it was useless. I was out of line for my actions, but I couldn't help it. This dude really had my nose open, his dope boy demeanor and boss mentality reminded me of Donk.

Knock! Knock! Knock!

Who the hell? I thought, reaching to the door.

I stood on the tips of my toes and peered out of the peephole. I jumped up and down in excitement before unlocking the locks.

"What's up?" he asked as soon as I snatch the door open.

"Where you been, Bando? I missed you," I whined wrapping my arms around his neck.

He squeezed me tightly as he hugged me back.

"What's wrong, baby?" I asked pulling away from his embrace.

He stepped inside and flopped down on the sofa while shaking his head in distress. "They hit the spot. I lost everything, Persuasia. I was finally a step away from being on top. I never been that close. What hurts the most is all the people I had to step on and over just to get there only to lose it all to a fuckboy."

"Wait a minute! What spot?"

"Come on, Persuasia now is not the time to play dumb."

"Nah, I just can't believe my ears," I admitted. Indeed, I was shocked seeing that it was so coincidental.

"So, where's Twan?"

"They shot and killed him." I placed my hand over my heart in disbelief. "And on top of that, someone murked Lil' Tim in the privacy of his home."

"*Tim?* Oh my God," I whispered peering at Bando dumbfounded.

I couldn't believe all the shit I was hearing that I knew nothing about. I reached out and caressed Bando's hand as I watched the teardrops roll down his face. He and Tim were closer than he and anyone else. Tim was the reason he came to Texas. I thought of a hundred different things I could do to ease Bando's mind, but I was afraid he would reject me. The last thing I wanted to do was force him to run off again. Bando had been the closest thing to Donk I'd found and I'd become dependent.

I find myself waiting quite often. Waiting on a text, a call, compliment, any form of affection, anything that compelled my insides to flutter. Doing what I did best I strutted toward Bando in an attempt to seduce him, wrapping my arms around his neck, I stood directly in front of him while peering into his eyes. Teary-eyed he tried matching my gaze.

"Bando," I whispered.

"Hmmm?" he moaned.

"Things are fucked up today but tomorrow's got to come."

He nodded his head and continued to peer down. I squatted down and planted kisses on his lips. In the beginning, he sat there motionless, but after the first couple kisses, he began to kiss me back, before long we were both on the floor racing to tear one another's clothes off. Not even a sock was left to keep my feet warm. I spread my legs and allowed Bando to release his frustrations in whichever hole he preferred to take advantage of. His dick was smaller than what I was used to, but as he began to learn my body the sex got better and better.

All last night I was restless even after a night of intoxicating sex with Bando. I laid beside him watching the numbers change on the clock, anticipating tomorrow. As soon as Bando gathered his things and left, I was right behind him.

"Bitch, where you at?" I asked pretending to be cool.

"I'm at Bry's house me and—"

Click!

Without allowing her to finish I placed my phone into my purse and sped to Bry's apartment. I tried remaining calm, but as soon as Shaniece answered the door I became upset all over again.

"Damn, what's up P?" Shaniece asked with a look of confusion on her face.

"Don't what's up, P me," I uttered calmly pressing my index finger into her forehead, as she backpedaled inside the apartment.

"Damn, bitch, what's up?"

"What's up? You a cut-throat ass bitch, that's what's up!" I yelled.

"Hold—" Bry started.

"Nah, fuck that Bry this bitch hit D—"

"Ssh! Ssh! Ssh!" Shaniece charged me placing her index fingers up to her lips.

"Nah, don't ssshhh me your family should know how dirty you is. Bry, I told this bitch not to hit Donk's spot and she did anyway!"

"No, I did not," Shaniece protested shaking her head.

"Quit lying, bro!"

"What it matter to you, anyway? Donk's fucking Esha!" she blasted.

I cut my eyes at Bry giving her a menacing scowl. She's the only person that could've told Shaniece that.

"I'm alright with him fucking Esha, cuz' I'm fucking Bando bitch! That's how I know the spot was hit cuz he told me but since you being extra—"

"Oh, so you fucking Bando?" Mun asked walking out of the kitchen with his brows raised, seeming surprisingly calm.

"What the?" I asked looking around frantically eyes big as golf balls.

"We tried to tell you," Shaniece and Bry spoke in unison.

"Bry, you knew all along your cousin hit my shit? After I just vented how upset I was and all along you knew the culprit?"

"*Culprit? Me?* Bry ass was with me!" Shaniece's dog ass yelled.

I gasped, I didn't think Bry would do something so ruggish.

"I knew you looked all too familiar," Mun spoke through clenched teeth before biting down on his lip.

He locked eyes with Bry and I could've sworn I saw a tear, but it vanished as fast as it came.

Boom! Boom!

The first bullet smashed into Shaniece's chest forcing her to apply pressure at the new wound. The second bullet hit her in the throat sending her face-first into the cheap carpet.

"Mun, please stop! Shaniece asked me to come but I swear I didn't know it was your brother's you have to believe me," Bry begged as tears streamed down her face and she spoke through sniffles.

"Nah, all y'all some set up bitches if you ask me. All three of you hoes in cahoots."

"What about Shania?" she asked through trembling lips.

Mun arms stiffened, his scowl softened for a moment and his shoulders sagged, but his arms never fell.

"I'll make sure she's good."

Boom! Like a sack of potatoes Bry's body hit the floor.

Boom! Boom!

Chapter 31

Donk

"Unc, where you going?" Kadejah and Arianna ask standing in the entryway of the study.

"Not far I'll be back. When I get there, I'll call. I'll only be gone for a few days," I answered.

A hundred thoughts were running through my mind. From the betrayal of Lil' Tim and now the big loss, complications of being a father, and the new territory we were about to step into. Most of all I wish my sister Quaylo was here, shit hasn't been right since she passed days after I was released.

"Watch out y'all. Hey, man you ready?" Mun asked drenched in sweat as he barged inside.

"Uncle Mun, I love you."

"Me too," Arianna agreed

"I love y'all too quit crying we not going to another planet. We'll be back. Why did you even tell them?" Mun asked.

"Kadejah's nosey ass overheard me talking to your ass on the phone." Mun rolled his eyes while he scanned the room. "You alright?" I asked eyeing him suspiciously.

"Yeah, I'm good. I'm just ready to go."

"I feel that, let's go. Hey, Dejah come here. Look while we gone, I need you to hold it down. Tim is gone and Bando is not to be trusted. I'm telling you this cause you solid. Age has nothing to do with it. I trust you, I raised you, so I know what you made of. I love you, hold it down."

Tears streamed down her face and I kissed her on the forehead before walking away.

"Arianna, I'm not mad at you. What's done is done. I just want you to do better," I admitted.

"Be safe and stay woke!" Mun yelled to the girls as we made our way outside.

The ride from Dallas to New Orleans was a pretty nice distance. I tried keeping my eyes open while Mun worked the wheel. I just couldn't believe how everything had changed so fast. Now it was a bunch of I *shouldas* floating around in my mind. I kept swallowing the lump every time it formed in my throat, but my thought never subsided like the saliva. For a long time, I moved careless and effortlessly because I was up one not in the terms of numbers, but levels.

I was ahead of the game now look at me, 8500 tucked away in my Louis Vuitton backpack as well as the two ounces of glass. On the hunt for half a bird, more than likely is going to be cut. That's how niggas do it nowadays. You'll rarely find something pure and uncut unless your plug's name is Lito. I miss doing business with Lito, but my past life fucked that up for Mun and I, years ago.

"Don't forget to hit the alarm," I told Mun before heading inside the small motel room. My mind was so cluttered, I didn't even know the name of the motel we were staying in. Mun hit the alarm as we headed inside. Mun hadn't spoken the entire drive. He must've been thinking how I was thinking. The room looked low budget but neat. I could tell it was a hole in the wall when I spotted the fat back on the T.V. Pawnshops don't even sell those anymore. Electronics don't come with baggage anymore, but who am I to gripe? I'm one wrong move away from being broke.

"Once we get the work, we'll get a door in those apartments on Loyola Avenue if shit jumping harder down here we'll stay another week," I said.

I dialed Kadejah's number and informed her of my whereabouts then sent my love to Arianna.

"You hear me?" I asked Mun.

"Yeah, yeah, my bad I was thinking about something."

"Man, bro come on, tell me what's on your mind. You know I know when you lying," I voiced.

Mun peered up at me lacking expression. The deadpan stare forced me to sit down because I knew it was something.

"I found the chick that robbed our spot and shot Twan."

"That's what's up! So, what's the issue? Where you find her?"

"She was with Bry and Persuasia."

"*Bry and Persuasia?*" I asked taken aback.

"Yeah, they were at Bry's house."

"Quit going in circles, tell me what's up," I said becoming frustrated.

"I killed all three of them," he whispered.

"You killed my baby momma, bro?" I asked through narrow slits.

"Yeah, she can't be trusted, fam."

"That's for me to decide! We shared a child. That's my bitch, separated or together."

"Come on, Donk. P.J.'s not even yours."

"He was mine. I raised him and took care of him. You was doing for Shania. You and Bry wasn't even rocking like that. I'm a real nigga if I love you, I love any and everyone you love."

"Well, you was gon' do it anyway."

"No, I wasn't, I love her too much despite what she did."

"Oh, yeah? Well, did you know she was fucking Bando? I heard it out of her own mouth."

"I knew that lil' nigga couldn't be trusted."

"Yo', bitch can't neither," Mun announced standing to his feet and walking out the door.

I couldn't believe Persuasia would do something so file. I removed my kicks and sat in the love seat in silence. I knew she would get me back for fucking Esha, but I didn't think she would go this far. Betraying me in the worst way didn't take any of the love I had stored up inside my heart for her. Even though I loved her, clearly, I had no plans on reviving the old flame. She hurt me in a way I'd never been hurt. When you can walk away from someone that you hold so close to heart because they're detrimental that's when you know you love yourself.

Boom! The sudden noise startled me, and I snatched the .45 from my waist only to be met by ten guns pointed at me.

"Police! Get the fuck down! Tell us where it's at to make it easy on yourself!" The white cop yelled with spit flying from his mouth.

I wanted to scream *"Fuck you!"* However, the state of shock disabled me from speaking.

"Grab that bag!" A different cop yelled.

My heart fell to my toes and I knew right then it was over.

"Cuff him," he demanded, tossing the dope to the officer standing behind him.

It's been a minute since I sat on the cold steel, but the feeling was all too familiar as if I'd never left. I hopped up and quickly dialed Mun's number on the open payphone while waiting to be booked in.

"Aye!" I yelled into the speaker

"Yeah, I'm here what the fuck happened?"

"That's what I'm trying to figure out. One minute I was chilling and the next minute I was cuffed."

"How much is your bond?"

"I don't know yet I'm waiting to get booked in, but look Steve's number is eight-one-seven-three-five-four-six-eight-two-eight call him and he'll know what to do."

"Okay, I'm about to do that, right now."

I flopped down onto the hard seat while giving Mun time to call Steve. I thought about the entire situation. We weren't wanted so we shouldn't have been followed. *Who is the rat?* I thought back to the argument Mun and I had before he stormed out. It was a coincidence they rolled in right after he left. I really didn't want to believe what I was thinking but the facts were in plain view. Twenty minutes had passed so I stood and dialed Mun's number.

"Hey, he said he got you don't worry. You have two charges pending. An unlawfully carrying weapon and possession charge. He'll be up there to visit you tomorrow if you're not already out."

"Okay, I'll call you again when I make it upstairs."

"Bet."

It didn't take long as I thought for me to get booked in and head upstairs. Despite the ugly orange scrubs I wore, the female C.O.s gawked at me lustfully as soon as I bent the corner. I went inside six tanks scanning the dorm for an empty cell. The gang of dudes in the dayroom looked at me like I was an outsider.

Come to think of it I was. The jail was set up different than the county in Dallas, but I didn't dwell on it too much. I met the eyes of the men who gawked until they felt uncomfortable and looked away. Luckily, the first cell was pretty empty, so I found a bunk and placed my mat on top of it. Without removing my sheets to cover the green mat. I laid on it as was. It was flat as a pancake, but I'd slept on tile floors when I was younger, so it wasn't nothing to gripe about.

I sat in the empty visitation booth waiting on Steve. I tried calling Mun three times yesterday, but he never picked up. I was already tripping now wasn't the time for him to ignore a nigga. I stood up and peered through the square-shaped glass on the other side of the window, but I didn't see any sign of Steve. I was still trying to wrap my mind around everything something wasn't right.

"Hey, Donk." Steve walked in.

"What's up, boy? What took you so long?"

"I forgot these and it's very important that you see it for yourself. So, I had to run back to my car. I was just so anxious to speak with you."

"See what?"

"I'll get to that. Your bond is set at one hundred and fifteen thousand dollars. I'm going to post it as soon as I leave here."

"You know I got you as soon as I get out."

"You've always had me, now I got you, it's cool."

"Have you talked to Mun?"

"He's not picking up. I was going to ask you the same thing."

I fiddled with the hairs on my chin as I begin to ponder on the possibility of Mun setting me up, but the thought died as soon as it was surfaced cause if no one had my back. Quaylo and Mun did.

"You have the motion of discovery?"

"Yes, I do," Steve answered with a hint of sorrow and disbelief on his face. "You're wanting to know who the rat is, huh?" he continued.

"Yeah."

"I'm going to flip through the pages for you and place it up to the glass, okay?"

"Come on with it," I agreed.

This must be some serious shit for Steve to do it this way instead of telling me. I scanned through the thick packet, but nothing exposed the identity of the informant.

"Steve fuck the irrelevant shit turn to the page where the name of the snitch is listed."

"You're looking at it read the bottom section."

"Nah, man na—" I stammered before I fell silent peering through wide eyes at the name on the page.

"It surprised the hell out of me too but it's in black and white, Donk."

"But, nah we, we better than that. How could—" I dropped my head in disbelief. My breathing had become irregular as I shook my head.

"Times up!" the C.O. yelled.

"I'm going now to post your bond. Don't do nothing crazy," Steve said standing to his feet.

I remained silent and seated. I was so distraught and stunned. *This shit right here is unbelievable.*

"Come on, sir," the C.O. demanded.

I slowly rose to my feet and headed back to my cell.

Chapter 32

Mun

I sat in the room awaiting Donk's call. I had even tried calling Steve, but he didn't answer. They both hit my line last night but, I was in no position to answer. I was dead smack in the middle of doing something I don't usually do. See back then Donk's preference was to jug. I sell dope and finesse. Over time Donk decided to switch things up, with him being locked up and the laws taking the last of cash and dope. I was forced to make a move. Not just any move last night I was out chasing that sack. I made it back to the room ten thousand dollars richer. So, now I was in a position to phone the plug to buy the dope.

Ring! Ring!

"Bro! Aye Donk."

"What's up? What time—"

"Look, Steve said he just tried post—"

"They calling me out. I'm being released I'll see you outside!"

"No! Lis—"

Click!

"Fuck!" I yelled pounding the steering wheel.

I hopped in the Nissan Altima and sped out the lot. I arrived at the jail in exactly sixteen minutes but there was no sign of Donk. I drove up and down the street hoping I would see him, but no luck there. I veered into the lot of a beer and wine store nearby I even peered inside but there was still no sign of him. I placed my foot on the pedal peering to the left and right. I scowled curiously when I thought I saw a slight movement to the left on the side of the store. I immediately hit the brakes, hopped out the whip, and instantly spotting a bloody Donk. He laid on his back clutching the wounds and choking on his own blood while blinking profusely.

I whipped out my phone and dialed 911 right away while jogging towards him.

"I'm across the street from the county jail at the beer and wine store. Please hurry my brother has been shot!" Without disconnecting the call, I slid it into my pocket just in case my directions weren't clear enough.

"Come on Fam we been through this shit before. You built for this shit, hang on for me."

He tightened his lips and I could feel his body tighten as well. I knew he was in an abundance of pain.

"Please, bruh, I need you. You all I got man," I spoke rocking back and forth as the salty liquid descended down my face and into the corners of my mouth.

I stared back at Donk while applying pressure to the wounds. It looked like he'd been hit four times, but I wasn't sure. I could hear sirens in the distance, and I begin to rock faster.

"Ta- ta- talk to—"

"Quit trying to talk just hold on."

"Listen," he whispered.

I knew he was in pain when his words were just barely over a whisper. "Talk to Steve," he strained to say.

"Load him on the gurney!" The paramedic yelled jumping out the back door of the van. I hopped in the back of the van instead of taking my car because I couldn't take the chance of losing Donk and being absent if he takes his last breath.

Chapter 33

Kadejah

The suspect had been identified for shooting uncle Donk. She wasn't even an hour away from the scene before she was arrested.

"I knew that bitch was up to something!" I yelled slamming my fist down on the coffee table as the picture of the weird lady who frequently visited the coffee shop popped up. Her name was unfamiliar, but I'd never forget her face or those eyes. I knew she wasn't continuously visiting to sample everything on the menu.

Caleb: //: R u home?

Me: //: Yes

I'm glad Caleb texted me so I could tell him that we could no longer see each other.

Caleb: //: I'm outside.

Me: //: Okay.

I quickly ran and opened the door for Caleb. He barged inside before I could say, "Hey."

"Look, I just want to—"

"Did you snitch on your uncle?"

"What? Where did that come from?" I asked.

"Did you, Kadejah?" he asked inching closer.

I became nervous, the D. A. promised he wouldn't leak the source. *They'll never forgive me,* I thought. Ashamed I dropped my head in defeat.

"You're pathetic, dawg! How could you snitch on your own blood for a bitch you hardly know? She's not loyal to you!"

"Yes, she is," I whispered.

"Oh, you sure of that?" Caleb sneered.

My heart began to race knowing he was about to drop the bomb on me.

"Arianna didn't tell you?"

"Tell me what?"

"They were fucking ironically they were roommates, too. C.O. Ms. Smith caught them the night before Arianna left. She has pictures of Arianna in her folder and letters."

That explains why she runs out and waits on the mailman every day, I thought.

"I dont believe you," I lied trying to save face.

"I knew you wouldn't that's why I took the initiative to bring this," he said holding up the sheet of paper.

"What's that?" I asked snatching the paper from his hand.

"A copy of the case."

It read: At 9:10 p.m. Lytrice Oshae was found in between the legs of Arianna Jenkins the two offenders were told to stop, which they did so immediately.

My hands trembled and my face became hot. I wanted to strangle Arianna's thin ass, but she had run out earlier with a friend. I peered up at Caleb through watery eyes and begin crying uncontrollably. Acting off instinct and what I thought was love is the reason my uncle is in the hospital fighting for his life.

"How did you know I snitched?"

"She's running around bragging about it."

"What am I going to do, Caleb?"

"Kadejah, I dont know," he replied shrugging his shoulders.

Chapter 34

Mun

I left Donk's side in the trauma room the doctor assured he would make it. Steve informed me about Kadejah's disloyalty. It surprised me because she was Quaylo's seed and Quaylo would have never done no shit like that. Not only that but, she was raised by the best, she knew better. There were certain things Donk and I instilled in her before she learned basic math. I shrugged it off and kept it moving. Even in the bible, in *Micah 7:5*, it states, *In the last days don't trust anyone, not a best friend, not even your wife.*

I left Donk when Steve phoned me and informed me of the culprit that shot Donk. She was waiting to be arraigned and I wanted to make sure this bitch got a bond, so I could post her bond and pop her ass like she did Donk. I rushed inside the courtroom and sat all the way at the back.

"What was this old lady's beef with Donk?" I asked myself. *Was she paid?* I thought.

"You know who that is, right?" I jumped at the sight of Steve standing behind me. "You not living right," he commented with a grin.

"Nigga you know I ain't living right, don't scare me like that again."

"Calm down," Steve said sitting down beside me grinning.

"Who is that?"

"That's the grandmother of your niece's victim."

"Huh?" I ask evidently dumbfounded.

"Remember when Kadejah stabbed the dude at the gas station?"

"Yeah, Meech."

"That's his grandmother."

"The sick old lady?"

"I don't know anything about her being sick she looks fine to me."

"Well, Donk, told me she was a sick elderly woman. I was completely appalled at the entire situation.

The judge entered clearing his throat. He rambled on and on, but I paid no attention. The gavel banging against the wood captured my attention.

"There will be no bond set at this time."

I glanced once more time at the old lady, this time we locked eyes. Her eyes grew twice the size as she gasped for air while frantically squirming around in the cuffs.

She noticed me, I thought.

She winced evidently at the pain and seconds later she collapsed.

"Code red we need medical," the C.O. shouted.

I turned and looked at Steve, no words were spoken as we slid out of our seats and eased out of the courtroom. The fresh breeze was like weave to a bald head chick.

"So, what's the plan?" Steve asked.

"I have to handle some unfinished business. I'll catch you later, Steve."

"Give me a call if you need me," he said

"You do the same," I replied heading in the direction of my car.

"Hey, Mun," Steve called out.

"What's up?" I answered turning around.

"Stay woke," he said.

I smirked as I proceeded to my car. *What the hell does Steve know about that?* I thought.

"Hey, I need to rap with you Fam. Donk's in the hospital let me in," I spoke in a concerned tone.

"*Hospital?* For what? Come on in. Where you at?" Bando asked peering out of the door. "Mun?" he yelled

"What's up," I answered popping out from the side of the house, Glock in hand pointed directly at his chest.

"What's this? What up, Fam?"

"Nigga, you know what it is back the fuck up," I demanded shoving the pistol in his chest as he backpedaled inside. Bando looked appalled at first but that terrified look was replaced with a mischievous smirk. "I knew you were on your way once Persuasia came up missing. I knew it was just a matter of time," Bando spoke.

"After everything this how you repay us, man?" I spoke through narrow slits and clenched teeth. I just couldn't fathom the mental of a snake. "Why bite the hand? Niggas just don't keep it real no more."

"Y'all don't give positions to the nigga that earns it. You give it to the ones you're closest to. You know you didn't deserve that second in command position. I did, that should've been me! I put blood, sweat, and tears into this shit while you were in Mexico eating tacos and shit!"

"Oh, so this about me?"

"Since you walked out of that hospital it's been about you."

"You the bitch that orchestrated that hit at the cemetery, huh? I knew it was an amateur," I said while smirking mischievously. "All this bloodshed over a position. If you would've just stayed down eventually there would've been a position for you."

"Nah, I'm not Fam. It would've been Lil' Tim then P.J." He stared back at me angrily. I stared back at him skeptically. "That's why I made that move with P.J."

"*P.J?* I thought that was Tim"

"Yeah, that was me and Mariyah's plan all along to blame Tim."

I instantly felt remorseful for Tim's death. He was truly a real one who lost his life behind some fuckery.

"Sometimes, Fam, good just ain't good enough."

Bam! Boom! Boom!

"Nigga you ain't my fam."

I entered Donk's room seeing that he was still asleep I inched closer. Seeing my nigga lying there with tubes down his throat saddened my spirit. I reached out and cradled his hand squeezing it just a little, wishing he'd squeeze mine back.

"I knew I'd find you here."

I didn't even have to turn around. The hairs on the back of my neck stood up once I heard Juanito's voice. I turned around to see him and three of his men at the door.

"Ah ah, ah, ah! Don't move, Mun."

Ah'Million

Fuck Juanito and whatever he was talking about. I continued to rest my hand on the Glock that was tucked in my waist. I didn't show it, but I was certainly upset with myself for allowing Juanito to catch me slipping. I visualized a sensible way out but shut it down. I hoped one of my guys would arrive, but I forgot they were all dead. It's crazy I had to kill niggas and bitches I thought had my best interest at heart.

I had to give it to Lil Tim. He was a real dude as well and died one. I wish things would've happened differently with him. Although, its only one nigga I trust wholeheartedly and that's the one on the side of me, Donk. Juanito removed the silencer. There was no way of escaping this usually, I'd still have hope knowing Donk was somewhere lurking, but truthfully Donk never made it.

He died as soon as we made it to the hospital. The doctor resuscitated him but, she said it was useless being that the oxygen machine was the only thing that was keeping him alive. I begged her not to pull the plug. I figured if I stayed, he'd live so I planned on camping out until they put me out. That's why I'm standing here now, cherishing these last moments, although I'm basically talking to a corpse. Once she assured me he was suffering I gave in, but I refused to leave his side.

Honestly, I don't mind dying today. At least I'd be with him, my mother and my sister. I have no other reason for living. Kadejah may need me, but after what she did to Donk. I lost a lot of love for her. Death has always found me and my circle. Kadejah would be safer without me. But without Donk who would keep me sane? Who would have my back? I've lost everything! Where's the love at? Love will get you killed. Donk is a prime example of that. I'm merely a lost cause. I just hope Heaven has room for two Gs. If not, I guess I'll be dancing with the devil.

I turned around and peered into Juanito's eyes. Like a bolt from above, I felt Donk squeeze my hand weakly. My eyes bucked, and I felt shock and fear all at once, as I quickly began to think of a way I could save both of us.

Psst! The first bullet hit me hard shifting my thoughts. I was too late. *Psst! Psst!* Things got dark and my whole life played back in highlighted segments. The wrong I'd done. The triumphs, the mistakes, and the failures. Everything, and then I crossed over into more darkness, but there was a glimmer of light up ahead.

The End!

Submission Guideline

Submit the first three chapters of your completed manuscript to ldpsubmissions@gmail.com, subject line: Your book's title. The manuscript must be in a .doc file and sent as an attachment. Document should be in Times New Roman, double spaced and in size 12 font. Also, provide your synopsis and full contact information. If sending multiple submissions, they must each be in a separate email.

Have a story but no way to send it electronically? You can still submit to LDP/Ca$h Presents. Send in the first three chapters, written or typed, of your completed manuscript to:

LDP: Submissions Dept
Po Box 944
Stockbridge, Ga 30281

DO NOT send original manuscript. Must be a duplicate.

Provide your synopsis and a cover letter containing your full contact information.

Thanks for considering LDP and Ca$h Presents.

Toe Tagz 3

Toe Tagz 3

Coming Soon from Lock Down Publications/Ca$h Presents

BOW DOWN TO MY GANGSTA
By **Ca$h**
TORN BETWEEN TWO
By **Coffee**
THE STREETS STAINED MY SOUL **II**
By **Marcellus Allen**
BLOOD OF A BOSS **VI**
SHADOWS OF THE GAME II
By **Askari**
LOYAL TO THE GAME **IV**
By **T.J. & Jelissa**
A DOPEBOY'S PRAYER **II**
By **Eddie "Wolf" Lee**
IF LOVING YOU IS WRONG… **III**
By **Jelissa**
TRUE SAVAGE **VII**
MIDNIGHT CARTEL III
DOPE BOY MAGIC IV
By **Chris Green**
BLAST FOR ME **III**
A SAVAGE DOPEBOY III
CUTTHROAT MAFIA II
By **Ghost**
A HUSTLER'S DECEIT III
KILL ZONE **II**
BAE BELONGS TO ME III
A DOPE BOY'S QUEEN II
By **Aryanna**

Ah'Million

CHAINED TO THE STREETS III

By **J-Blunt**

COKE KINGS V

KING OF THE TRAP II

By **T.J. Edwards**

GORILLAZ IN THE BAY V

TEARS OF A GANGSTA II

De'Kari

THE STREETS ARE CALLING II

Duquie Wilson

KINGPIN KILLAZ IV

STREET KINGS III

PAID IN BLOOD III

CARTEL KILLAZ IV

DOPE GODS II

Hood Rich

SINS OF A HUSTLA II

ASAD

TRIGGADALE III

Elijah R. Freeman

KINGZ OF THE GAME V

Playa Ray

SLAUGHTER GANG IV

RUTHLESS HEART IV

By **Willie Slaughter**

THE HEART OF A SAVAGE III

By **Jibril Williams**

FUK SHYT II

By **Blakk Diamond**

THE DOPEMAN'S BODYGAURD II

By Tranay Adams

TRAP GOD II

By Troublesome

YAYO III

A SHOOTER'S AMBITION III

By S. Allen

GHOST MOB

Stilloan Robinson

KINGPIN DREAMS II

By Paper Boi Rari

CREAM

By Yolanda Moore

SON OF A DOPE FIEND II

By Renta

FOREVER GANGSTA II

GLOCKS ON SATIN SHEETS II

By Adrian Dulan

LOYALTY AIN'T PROMISED II

By Keith Williams

THE PRICE YOU PAY FOR LOVE II

DOPE GIRL MAGIC II

By Destiny Skai

CONFESSIONS OF A GANGSTA II

By Nicholas Lock

I'M NOTHING WITHOUT HIS LOVE II

By Monet Dragun

CAUGHT UP IN THE LIFE II

By Robert Baptiste

NEW TO THE GAME III

By **Malik D. Rice**

Ah'Million

LIFE OF A SAVAGE III
By **Romell Tukes**
QUIET MONEY II
By **Trai'Quan**
THE STREETS MADE ME II
By **Larry D. Wright**
THE ULTIMATE SACRIFICE VI
By **Anthony Fields**
THE LIFE OF A HOOD STAR
By Ca$h & Rashia Wilson

Available Now

RESTRAINING ORDER **I & II**
By **CA$H & Coffee**
LOVE KNOWS NO BOUNDARIES **I II & III**
By **Coffee**
RAISED AS A GOON I, II, III & IV
BRED BY THE SLUMS I, II, III
BLAST FOR ME I & II
ROTTEN TO THE CORE I II III
A BRONX TALE I, II, III
DUFFEL BAG CARTEL I II III IV
HEARTLESS GOON I II III IV
A SAVAGE DOPEBOY I II
HEARTLESS GOON I II III
DRUG LORDS I II III
CUTTHROAT MAFIA

Toe Tagz 3

By **Ghost**
LAY IT DOWN **I & II**
LAST OF A DYING BREED
BLOOD STAINS OF A SHOTTA I & II III
By **Jamaica**
LOYAL TO THE GAME I II III
LIFE OF SIN I, II III
By **TJ & Jelissa**
BLOODY COMMAS I & II
SKI MASK CARTEL I II & III
KING OF NEW YORK I II,III IV V
RISE TO POWER I II III
COKE KINGS I II III IV
BORN HEARTLESS I II III IV
KING OF THE TRAP
By **T.J. Edwards**
IF LOVING HIM IS WRONG…I & II
LOVE ME EVEN WHEN IT HURTS I II III
By **Jelissa**
WHEN THE STREETS CLAP BACK I & II III
THE HEART OF A SAVAGE I II
By **Jibril Williams**
A DISTINGUISHED THUG STOLE MY HEART I II & III
LOVE SHOULDN'T HURT I II III IV
RENEGADE BOYS I II III IV
PAID IN KARMA I II III
By **Meesha**
A GANGSTER'S CODE I &, II III
A GANGSTER'S SYN I II III
THE SAVAGE LIFE I II III

Ah'Million

CHAINED TO THE STREETS I II
By J-Blunt
PUSH IT TO THE LIMIT
By **Bre' Hayes**
BLOOD OF A BOSS **I, II, III, IV, V**
SHADOWS OF THE GAME
By **Askari**
THE STREETS BLEED MURDER **I, II & III**
THE HEART OF A GANGSTA I II& III
By **Jerry Jackson**
CUM FOR ME I II III IV V
An **LDP Erotica Collaboration**
BRIDE OF A HUSTLA **I II & II**
THE FETTI GIRLS **I, II& III**
CORRUPTED BY A GANGSTA I, II III, IV
BLINDED BY HIS LOVE
THE PRICE YOU PAY FOR LOVE
DOPE GIRL MAGIC
By **Destiny Skai**
WHEN A GOOD GIRL GOES BAD
By **Adrienne**
THE COST OF LOYALTY I II III
By Kweli
A GANGSTER'S REVENGE **I II III & IV**
THE BOSS MAN'S DAUGHTERS I II III IV V
A SAVAGE LOVE **I & II**
BAE BELONGS TO ME I II
A HUSTLER'S DECEIT I, II, III
WHAT BAD BITCHES DO I, II, III
SOUL OF A MONSTER I II III

KILL ZONE

A DOPE BOY'S QUEEN

By **Aryanna**

A KINGPIN'S AMBITON

A KINGPIN'S AMBITION **II**

I MURDER FOR THE DOUGH

By **Ambitious**

TRUE SAVAGE I II III IV V VI

DOPE BOY MAGIC I, II, III

MIDNIGHT CARTEL I II

By **Chris Green**

A DOPEBOY'S PRAYER

By **Eddie "Wolf" Lee**

THE KING CARTEL **I, II & III**

By **Frank Gresham**

THESE NIGGAS AIN'T LOYAL **I, II & III**

By **Nikki Tee**

GANGSTA SHYT **I II &III**

By **CATO**

THE ULTIMATE BETRAYAL

By **Phoenix**

BOSS'N UP **I , II & III**

By **Royal Nicole**

I LOVE YOU TO DEATH

By Destiny J

I RIDE FOR MY HITTA

I STILL RIDE FOR MY HITTA

By **Misty Holt**

LOVE & CHASIN' PAPER

By **Qay Crockett**

Ah'Million

TO DIE IN VAIN
SINS OF A HUSTLA
By **ASAD**
BROOKLYN HUSTLAZ
By **Boogsy Morina**
BROOKLYN ON LOCK I & II
By **Sonovia**
GANGSTA CITY
By **Teddy Duke**
A DRUG KING AND HIS DIAMOND I & II III
A DOPEMAN'S RICHES
HER MAN, MINE'S TOO I, II
CASH MONEY HO'S
By Nicole Goosby
TRAPHOUSE KING **I II & III**
KINGPIN KILLAZ I II III
STREET KINGS I II
PAID IN BLOOD **I II**
CARTEL KILLAZ I II III
DOPE GODS
By **Hood Rich**
LIPSTICK KILLAH **I, II, III**
CRIME OF PASSION I II & III
By **Mimi**
STEADY MOBBN' **I, II, III**
THE STREETS STAINED MY SOUL
By **Marcellus Allen**
WHO SHOT YA **I, II, III**
SON OF A DOPE FIEND
Renta

220

GORILLAZ IN THE BAY **I II III IV**

TEARS OF A GANGSTA

DE'KARI

TRIGGADALE I II

Elijah R. Freeman

GOD BLESS THE TRAPPERS I, II, III

THESE SCANDALOUS STREETS I, II, III

FEAR MY GANGSTA I, II, III

THESE STREETS DON'T LOVE NOBODY I, II

BURY ME A G I, II, III, IV, V

A GANGSTA'S EMPIRE I, II, III, IV

THE DOPEMAN'S BODYGAURD

Tranay Adams

THE STREETS ARE CALLING

Duquie Wilson

MARRIED TO A BOSS... I II III

By Destiny Skai & Chris Green

KINGZ OF THE GAME I II III IV

Playa Ray

SLAUGHTER GANG I II III

RUTHLESS HEART I II III

By Willie Slaughter

FUK SHYT

By Blakk Diamond

DON'T F#CK WITH MY HEART I II

By Linnea

ADDICTED TO THE DRAMA I II III

By Jamila

YAYO I II

A SHOOTER'S AMBITION I II

Ah'Million

By S. Allen
TRAP GOD
By Troublesome
FOREVER GANGSTA
GLOCKS ON SATIN SHEETS
By Adrian Dulan
TOE TAGZ I II III
By Ah'Million
KINGPIN DREAMS
By Paper Boi Rari
CONFESSIONS OF A GANGSTA
By Nicholas Lock
I'M NOTHING WITHOUT HIS LOVE
By Monet Dragun
CAUGHT UP IN THE LIFE
By Robert Baptiste
NEW TO THE GAME I II
By **Malik D. Rice**
Life of a Savage I II
By **Romell Tukes**
LOYALTY AIN'T PROMISED
By Keith Williams
Quiet Money
By **Trai'Quan**
THE STREETS MADE ME
By **Larry D. Wright**
THE ULTIMATE SACRIFICE I, II, III, IV, V
KHADIFI
By **Anthony Fields**
THE LIFE OF A HOOD STAR

222

Toe Tagz 3

By Ca$h & Rashia Wilson

<u>BOOKS BY LDP'S CEO, CA$H</u>

<u>TRUST IN NO MAN</u>
<u>TRUST IN NO MAN 2</u>
<u>TRUST IN NO MAN 3</u>
<u>BONDED BY BLOOD</u>
<u>SHORTY GOT A THUG</u>
<u>THUGS CRY</u>
<u>THUGS CRY 2</u>
<u>THUGS CRY 3</u>
<u>TRUST NO BITCH</u>
<u>TRUST NO BITCH 2</u>
<u>TRUST NO BITCH 3</u>
<u>TIL MY CASKET DROPS</u>
<u>RESTRAINING ORDER</u>
<u>RESTRAINING ORDER 2</u>
<u>IN LOVE WITH A CONVICT</u>
<u>LIFE OF A HOOD STAR</u>

<u>Coming Soon</u>
BONDED BY BLOOD 2
BOW DOWN TO MY GANGSTA

Toe Tagz 3

www.ingramcontent.com/pod-product-compliance
Lightning Source LLC
Chambersburg PA
CBHW070453260626
47161CB00004B/1289